Lead for Breakfast?

Longarm rose quietly in the dark room and dressed. As he strapped his gunbelt around his waist and headed for the door, Meg stirred.

"Longarm?" she said drowsily, still almost asleep.

"Yeah?"

"Thank you."

Longarm went back and kissed her warm, soft cheek. "My honor as well as my pleasure."

"You'll find him?" she asked, opening her eyes and gazing up at him gravely. "Des's killer."

"Count on it."

He kissed her cheek once more and then strode out of the bedroom into the sitting room. He retrieved his rifle from where he'd leaned it against the wall by the door, and left.

He'd no sooner drawn the door closed behind him than something cold, round, and hard was pressed behind his right ear. There was the crisp, decisive sound of a gun hammer being ratcheted back.

"I'm about to save this town a whole lot of misery," a raspy voice said into the same ear . . .

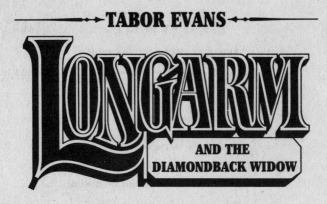

TABOR EVANS

LONGARM

AND THE
DIAMONDBACK WIDOW

JOVE BOOKS, NEW YORK

THE BERKLEY PUBLISHING GROUP
Published by the Penguin Group
Penguin Group (USA) Inc.
375 Hudson Street, New York, New York 10014, USA

USA | Canada | UK | Ireland | Australia | New Zealand | India | South Africa | China

Penguin Books Ltd., Registered Offices: 80 Strand, London WC2R 0RL, England
For more information about the Penguin Group, visit penguin.com.

LONGARM AND THE DIAMONDBACK WIDOW

A Jove Book / published by arrangement with the author

Jove Books are published by The Berkley Publishing Group.
JOVE® is a registered trademark of Penguin Group (USA) Inc.
The "J" design is a trademark of Penguin Group (USA) Inc.

For information, address: The Berkley Publishing Group,
a division of Penguin Group (USA) Inc.,
375 Hudson Street, New York, New York 10014.

ISBN: 978-0-515-15376-7

PUBLISHING HISTORY
Jove mass-market edition / August 2013

PRINTED IN THE UNITED STATES OF AMERICA

10 9 8 7 6 5 4 3 2 1

Cover illustration by Milo Sinovcic.

ALWAYS LEARNING   PEARSON

Chapter 1

Dan Garvey shook his head as he said, "They ought not to have done that. No sir, Sheriff Rainey—they ought not to have killed them poor people!"

"What're you talkin' about, Dan?" the sheriff said, bringing his buckskin to a halt on the desert trail in front of Garvey's old mule. "Who killed who?"

"Calvin didn't say?"

Des Rainey shook his head. "He just came into the office bright and early this morning and said you wanted to meet me about something important—a matter of life and death, he said—out here at the Diamondback Springs crossroads. Then he turned heel so fast that he damn near left his boots in my office and bolted off for the Dragoon Saloon."

"Goddamnit—I told Calvin no drinkin' in town! I told him to just deliver the dadgummed message to you at the sheriff's office and to head right on back to the ranch!"

"Dan," Sheriff Rainey said wearily, lifting his red neckerchief to mop sweat and dust from his brow. "Please tell me what poor people you think were murdered. That's why I rode all the way out here from Diamondback, after all."

The sheriff squinted a washed-out blue eye at the brassy sun hovering over the mountains in the west.

It was hot out here on the desert flats south of the Ramparts, the sun straight up in the air. It would be a good several hours before it got any cooler.

The heat was hard on a man the sheriff's age. Des Rainey was sixty years old and due to retire. The only problem was he didn't have the money to retire. He probably had enough for himself, but not enough for both him and his wife, Meg. He wanted to provide a good life as long as he could for the girl, almost half his age.

Fortunately, the town of Diamondback and the entire Rampart County had been relatively quiet since the Sioux had been run to ground by the U.S. Army. So quiet, in fact, that Rainey couldn't quite wrap his mind around the idea that someone had been murdered out here near Diamondback Springs.

"It's the Bear-Runners, Sheriff!" Dan Garvey threw an arm out to his right, pointing to a line of cottonwoods running along the base of the chalky buttes where Rainey knew that the spring-fed Diamondback Creek ran.

Squinting south, Rainey thought he could see tendrils of black smoke rising among the dusty trees, around where the Bear-Runner place sat, on the other side of a low rise.

A cold stone dropped in Rainey's belly as he turned his sorrel onto the trail that led south. He kicked the gelding into a trot, his eyes riveted on what could only be smoke rising through the cottonwoods. Garvey put his mule onto the trail behind Rainey, and the beast gave an anxious bray. Apparently, it didn't care to head back toward the Bear-Runner place.

Rainey felt the sorrel's muscles tighten beneath the saddle. The horse could smell the smoke and maybe something more that it didn't like any more than Garvey's mule did.

"Sarah seen the smoke last night," said Garvey, who had a small ranch about three miles up the creek from the Bear-Runner place. "I didn't get home from pushin' my beeves into the Ramparts till late, but Calvin an' me headed out this way first thing this mornin' to investigate."

Calvin Johnson was Garvey's only hired hand. Garvey had had a son old enough to wrangle cows and horses, but the poor boy had been killed when a rough-string bronc had thrown him against a gatepost. Now Garvey just lived on his little shotgun ranch with his second wife, Sarah, their baby, and their hired hand, Johnson.

Rainey rode up and over the low rise. As he started down the other side, he checked the sorrel down, and as Garvey stopped his mule beside him, the sheriff cast his gaze through the thin cottonwoods and across the narrow, meandering stream toward a ranch house sitting on the stream's far side, about seventy yards back from the water, in a little horseshoe gap in the chalky buttes.

Now it was no longer a ranch house, Rainey thought, heart thudding. Now it was merely a pile of charred, smoldering logs.

Rainey yelled, "Hee-yahh!" then whipped the sorrel's right hip with his rein ends and galloped on down the rise and through the cottonwoods. The gelding splashed across the stream, as did Garvey's mule, and thudded up the opposite bank and into the barren yard.

Rainey stared at the Bear-Runner's log cabin that looked as though it had been split down the middle by a giant, burning axe. The front wall was partly intact, though the roof and the bulk of the other three walls were burned to smoking ash-gray and black mounds. The large stone hearth stood against the remains of the right wall, also badly fire-blackened.

Two corrals stood to the right of the cabin. The barn was behind the corrals, as were a couple of other small log outbuildings and a farm wagon. The barn had been burned, though the corrals and the wagon appeared to have been untouched by the flames.

None of that interested Rainey.

The sheriff's attention was glued to the two charred bodies visible through the gray tendrils of wafting, fog-like smoke. One body lay in the yard. Another hung half out a front window to the left of the still-closed, halved-log front door that had a board nailed across it, locking it from the outside. Both people were so badly burned that it was impossible to distinguish their sexes, much less which members of the Bear-Runner family they were.

The family included the full-blood Hunkapa Sioux

Bear-Runner himself; his half-breed wife, Pearl; and their two sons, Nathaniel and George. They were wild horse hunters who also ran a few beeves, and Bear-Runner had been known to pan for gold, as well. The corral gates were open. It looked like someone had run off the Bear-Runner stock.

Rainey swung down from his jittery mount's back. He raised his neckerchief to his nose. The stench of burned logs and flesh was nearly palpable, causing Rainey's eyes to sting as he moved slowly toward the body lying in the yard before him.

He dropped to a knee beside the fire-blackened corpse, put his gloved hand to a shoulder, and rolled the body over. There wasn't much left of her face or her hair, but he could tell that the corpse belonged to Pearl Bear-Runner. A pasty black substance oozed out of her middle. She'd been shot.

"The woman?" Garvey asked, still sitting atop his mule and holding his forearm across his nose and mouth.

Rainey nodded. Feeling sick, he walked over to the second body, hanging out the window left of the door. Rainey dropped to a knee to the right of the corpse and lowered his head to angle a look up at the face.

This corpse wasn't in much better shape than Pearl's, but despite the long, charred black hair hanging straight down to the ground with the outstretched arms, Rainey could tell it was one of the boys—either George or Nathaniel. In the three years that the Bear-Runner family had lived out here, Rainey had seen the boys only a couple of times in town, but even if he'd known them well, it would have been impossible to tell which one this was, so badly burned was this young man's face.

"How do you suppose they got there?" Garvey asked, his voice muffled by his arm. Rainey's sorrel sidled away from the cabin, wickering its distaste for the stench. The horse started to head back toward the creek, but Garvey reached over and grabbed its bridle.

Rainey straightened and pondered the body hanging out the window. "Looks like they were shot inside the cabin. Someone set it on fire from inside, locked the shutters, nailed that board across the door. Pearl and the boy must've had enough life left in 'em to bust out. Only they were on fire by the time they finally got out. Died right here. Poor folks." The sheriff made a face and shook his head, deeply grieved. "Who on earth would do this?"

"Suppose the other two are still inside," Garvey said gravely.

Rainey didn't answer that. Instead, he walked around the cabin's left side, peering over what remained of the charred wall to inspect the inside. He could make out bits and pieces of the Bear-Runners' crudely fashioned but sturdy furniture and a black range, some pots and pans. He identified a broken hurricane lamp and part of a snowshoe that lay on the floor near the seat and arm of a burned, broken rocking chair.

Near the rocking chair was what at first glance looked like a tree branch jutting up from a mound of gray and black ashes, but which Rainey realized, after a closer look, was in fact a burned human arm. The outstretched hand had a charred gold ring on its ring finger. Rainey remembered seeing a thick gold ring on Bear-Runner's finger and vaguely thinking it odd to see such a white man's ornament adorning a full-blooded Indian's hand.

Seeing the ring stung Rainey, filled his belly with even more bile. The ring seemed to make the murders here—and what else could they be?—even more definite and real, in a surreal sort of way, than had the badly burned, unidentifiable bodies he'd already seen. The fact was he'd liked Bear-Runner, and he was genuinely sad to see to see the man and his family come to this.

Rainey continued walking to the back of the cabin. He was looking around at the ground for tracks between the singed sage clumps and rocks. There were plenty—boot prints as well a woman's shoe prints and horse tracks. Impossible to distinguish one man's prints from another's, though the tracks of whoever had killed the Bear-Runners had to be here somewhere.

The sheriff walked off behind the cabin, past a privy and a woodshed and an old, orange-painted farm wagon flanking the privy. Rainey knew the Bear-Runners had hauled firewood in the wagon. They often hauled a few loads to town in the fall to sell to the banker, Alexander Richmond, and attorney Charles Mulligan as well as a few other local mucky-mucks who could afford to hire their firewood cut and stacked for them, so they wouldn't have to get their hands dirty or endure a backache.

Rainey snorted at his own sour grapes. He was too old to harbor grudges against men better off than he. He'd never made much money and that had never bothered him—he'd enjoyed life anyway—until he'd been fortunate enough to marry a beautiful woman whom he loved and who loved him back.

Having a woman to provide for made money seem a whole lot more valuable . . .

Rainey walked around the burned barn and the corrals, looking for tracks. He didn't see any that stuck out from the others. But then, walking around behind the corral, he spied something on the ground between a small sage and a yucca plant. He stooped and picked up the cartridge casing.

A Spencer .56.

He frowned as he rolled the brass casing between his thumb and index finger. A common enough cartridge, though most men carried .44 Winchesters these days.

"Most men," the sheriff muttered, looking thoughtfully into the distance beyond the casing in his hand.

"Sheriff!"

Garvey's voice caused Rainey to drop the cartridge. Her jerked to his left, the direction from which the shout had come.

"What is it?"

"Oh, Jesus," Garvey screamed. There was a slight pause, and then the rancher's voice rose again—strained, garbled, as though he were out of breath or throwing up. "Come . . . come quick, Rainey. Hurry!"

Chapter 2

Smith & Wesson .44 in his hand, Des Rainey ran
between the breaking corral and the mounded rubble
of the burned barn and into the yard.

He followed Garvey's screams, now to his right,
running nearly straight out behind the cabin, past Garvey's mule that stood, reins drooping, fidgeting and
stomping around near where the ground sloped into a
ravine.

Garvey stopped at the lip of the ravine, which
appeared to be a former creek bed. It was littered with
rocks, old leaves, and branches that had fallen from
the cottonwoods and aspens on both sides of it.

Garvey was at the bottom of the ravine, looking up
at something hanging from a stout cottonwood branch
arcing over the dry creek bottom. Rainey walked
slowly down the slope, staring at a pair of well-worn
boots hanging suspended above the creek bed. The
boots twisted and turned slowly in the slight, hot

breeze, the tarnished brass spurs flashing dully in the sunlight filtering through the treetops.

Feeling his heartbeat increasing, the sheriff slid his gaze up from the boots, to a pair of patched, faded denim jeans . . . to a wide, black belt . . . to a coarse wool work shirt and red neckerchief . . . to a dark copper face and droopy eyelids. The skin stretched across the high-tapering cheekbones and the thin, black mustache mantling the full upper lip were those of a young man.

A boy of maybe sixteen, seventeen years old.

One of the Bear-Runner boys, obviously.

Rainey had been staring at the boy instead of his path down the steep, leaf-strewn slope. His left boot slipped out from beneath him, and he hit the ground with a loud grunt on his butt.

"Shit!"

Garvey started walking toward the sheriff, eyes still stricken with his grizzly find. "Shit, you all right, Rainey?"

The sheriff cursed again as he rose to his feet and walked more carefully to the creek bottom, flushed with embarrassment and wincing at the pain in his tailbone. You old son of a bitch, he heard his inner voice castigate him. Why don't you just retire, for Christ-fuckin'-sakes?

Garvey stepped back, regarding the sheriff uncertainly before lifting his chin toward the boy hanging from the tree.

"George Bear-Runner," Garvey breathed. He clucked and shook his head. "Sure as shit."

Rainey walked up to within a foot of the boots that

hung level with his nose. He looked the body over closely, walking around to inspect the dead boy's backside.

"No wounds," Rainey said.

He walked around to the front and inspected the boy's face. The Bear-Runner boy had a split lip and a swelling around his right eye. Several buttons of his shirt were gone, exposing part of a threadbare long-handle top.

He'd been roughed up before he'd been hanged. He'd likely been led out from the house by one man while another shot the kid's family and burned the cabin.

"Why?" Rainey said, lower jaw hanging, as he stared incredulously up at the hanged half-breed boy.

He turned to Garvey. "Who would do this, Dan? Who had it in for these people?"

A shadow moved on the slope of the ravine behind the rancher. As Garvey turned to Rainey, slowly shaking his head and opening his mouth to speak, the sheriff sprang forward, shouting, "Look out, Dan!"

He bulled into the rancher, knocking him off his feet. Garvey yelled as he hit the ground on his back, Rainey on top of him. At the same time, a rifle thundered loudly.

The slug plunked into the left shin of the hanging Bear-Runner boy, nudging the body sideways. Rainey rolled off of Garvey and raised his Smith & Wesson, aiming at the shadowy figure bounding out from behind a tree halfway down the southern slope and scrambling up toward the ridge.

The sheriff's revolver belched twice, his slugs merely pluming dust and leaves at the bushwhacker's heels. He fired again, but the bullet merely plinked a tree as the shooter ran up and over the ridge crest.

"Jesus Christ—what was that?" Garvey shouted.

"Stay here, Dan!"

Rainey heaved himself to his feet and started running up the southern ridge. Halfway to the top, he had to pause and catch his breath. His chest ached and his throat was dry.

Good Lord, he hoped he wasn't about to have a heart seizure!

He drew a deep breath and continued climbing until he was within a few feet of the top of the ridge. He slowed his pace, breathing hard and holding the S&W straight out in front of him, edging a cautious look over the brow of the hill.

Seeing nothing but the few shrubs and yucca plants capping the slope, he continued to the top. From somewhere ahead, a horse whinnied. As hooves began thudding hard, Rainey ran straight south along the bluff and stopped, casting his gaze down the far side.

A rider was galloping away on a dun horse through a crease in the buttes, his elbows and saddlebags flapping like wings. Crouched low over his horse's neck, the bushwhacker held a rifle in his right hand.

"Hold it!" Rainey shouted, dropping to one knee.

The rider kept galloping away.

Rainey extended the pistol in both hands, taking hasty aim at the jostling figure, and fired twice. Both slugs landed far short of the quickly receding rider.

He fired once more. The bullet spanged benignly off a rock well behind the man.

Rainey cursed and lowered the weapon, holding his

gaze on the rider, unable to make out much more about him than that he wore denims, a cream hat, a cream shirt, and a brown vest. He had short hair—hard to tell what color from this distance. He rode a dun horse with three white stockings. Nothing else he could see of the man distinguished him. Rainey did not recognize the horse.

When he was a hundred yards away, the bushwhacker looked back over his shoulder toward Rainey, but he was too far away for the sheriff to tell anything about his face. Frustrated, Rainey looked around carefully, making sure there were no other bushwhackers out there, and then he holstered his weapon and walked back down the ravine to where Dan Garvey was on one knee, looking nervous.

"You get him, Sheriff?"

Rainey shook his head and looked up at the dead Bear-Runner boy, who was partly turned away from him. The boy's long, blue-black hair blew in the breeze that funneled down the ravine. The rope creaked softly.

"You see who it was?"

"No."

Garvey straightened, adjusted his funnel-brimmed Stetson on his head, and brushed his wrist across his short, blunt nose. "Why the hell you suppose he was shooting at us?"

Rainey felt the frustration well inside him. "Dan, you're askin' too many questions—you know that? Just too damn many questions."

The truth was, Rainey himself was asking himself all the same questions, only he wasn't giving himself any answers.

He walked over to where the hanging rope had been tied off around a low branch, and said, "Let's get this poor boy down and dig us some graves."

It was late in the day when Rainey tossed the last shovelful of dirt on the grave of the elder Bear-Runner.

All four bodies were buried side by side on a little knoll north of the burned cabin, overlooking the creek. The sheriff thought the Bear-Runner family would have a nice rest there. At least, as nice a rest as anyone could have, having been shot and burned in their own cabin.

Or hanged from a tree in their backyard . . .

Rainey sighed as he leaned on his shovel and looked toward the burned out, still-smoldering hovel. Garvey was sitting on a nearby rock, smoking and looking as tired as Rainey felt after pulling the bodies out of the rubble and digging four graves on a hot, late-summer day in the high desert country of central Wyoming.

Clouds were building, as they often did in the afternoon this time of year. Large, angry, brooding clouds moving in fast on a cooling western breeze that rattled the leaves of cottonwoods and aspens down along Diamondback Creek.

"Who do you think done it, Sheriff?" Garvey asked, sweeping his gray-flecked sandy hair back from his sharp widow's peak and blowing out a long plume of cigarette smoke. "Who would've done such a thing? The Bear-Runners—they may have been Injuns, but they left folks alone. They went about their own business. Sure, Tanner Webster claimed they long-looped a few of his beeves, but just between you an' me, that could've been anyone. Tanner just assumed the Bear-Runners done it 'cause they were Injun."

Rainey pondered that information and then he let it go. Leaning on the shovel, he tended a bad feeling inside him.

He looked at Garvey. "Dan, did you know either one of the Bear-Runner boys to go to town much?"

Garvey stitched his brows together and then shook his head slowly. "Nah, I never seen 'em in town. That said, I don't get to town all that often myself. I never knew those boys to frequent the watering holes in Diamondback, though." Keeping his brows knitted, he studied Rainey. "Why do you ask?"

"Ah, hell, I don't know." Rainey looked at the clouds that were turning the late afternoon to an early dusk. "You'd better get on back to your ranch, and I'd best hit the trail for town, Dan. Gonna be rainin' soon. Thanks for letting me know about this, and for your help buryin' these poor people."

"Don't mention it, Sheriff. I'm torn up about it, myself." Garvey was walking beside Rainey as they headed for where they'd hobbled their mounts in the grass by the creek. "Just don't understand who could kill a whole family like that. Shoot 'em an' burn 'em . . . hang one of 'em. It's just like what happened east of the pass, three years back . . ."

As the two men swung into their saddles, Garvey turned to Rainey once more. "Hangin's usually done for folks caught rustlin', Sheriff."

Rainey nodded. "Yeah, it is."

"You think maybe George was caught rustlin' and

whoever owned the beef he rustled made his whole family pay?" Garvey winced at the thought.

"Could be," Rainey said. But he didn't think so. He gigged his horse across the creek. "Thanks again, Dan. I'll be checkin' in with you again soon."

"See ya, Sheriff," the rancher said as he turned his mule southwest along an old horse path that ran along the creek.

Rainey followed the secondary trail northwest to the main trail and then headed east toward Diamondback. He was so busy pondering the situation and tending that raw, burning feeling inside him that he wasn't aware it was storming until his sorrel started at a nearby thunderclap.

Lightning flashed on Rainey's right, flickering across the sky like two witches' fingers. The twin bolts hammered the top of a bluff on the far side of the creek, blowing up dirt and rock from a clump of boulders and causing a small rockslide.

It had been raining up to then, though Rainey had been only vaguely aware of the drops splattering his face. But now it was like a dam had broken loose, and the rain came in cold, white, buffeting sheets out of a sky the color of ripe plums. The sorrel whinnied and shook its mane but kept jogging up the winding trail that rose slowly toward Diamondback.

By the time the town appeared in a broad flat in the middle of the mountain-ringed basin, horse and rider were thoroughly soaked and mud-splattered. The horse was in a hurry to get in out of the rain. Rainey was, too, but he'd had a long think on his way into town and had more pressing business first.

He rode through town along its soupy main street to the other, eastern end of the modest little settlement. On the street's right side sat the long, low, mud-brick, brush-roofed building that was the Diamondback depot for the Wyoming Stage Company and also housed a telegraph and the local post office. Beyond the building was nothing but sage, yucca, prickly pear, and piñon pines studding the mountains all the way to Chugwater on the Wyoming-Dakota border.

Rainey put the sorrel up under the roof overhang, so that the cascade of rainwater missed the mount's hindquarters by a foot or two, and swung down from the leather.

He flung the reins over the hitchrack and then walked up onto the long front porch built of unpeeled pine poles, where he gave the closed plank door a tap and then tripped the string latch and pushed inside.

"Edgar, you here?" he called into the dingy shadows, his soaked clothes hanging on him.

A gravelly voice rose on the sheriff's left. "For cryin' out loud, Des, you don't have to scream at me! I'm sittin' right here and I may be hard of hearin' but I ain't deaf!"

Rainey turned to his left. Edgar Winthrop sat at one of the depot's long, pine-log tables, smoking a cigarette, a steaming mug of coffee on the table before him. A liver-colored cat stood atop the table, near the coffee cup and an open newspaper. It arched its back owlishly at the stranger who'd burst into the building unannounced and likely disturbed its nap there atop the newspaper.

"Sorry, Edgar," Rainey said, doffing his hat and

wincing when a cupful of water sluiced off its crown and its brim to splash the scuffed pine floor at his soaked boots. "I'm just wonderin' if you can send a message to Denver for me."

The gray-bearded old depot agent/telegrapher/post-master shook his head as he drew on his hand-rolled quirley, the coal glowing in the room's near-darkness. The rain hammered on the roof, punctuated by frequent thunder booms and the heels of lightning flashing in the windows.

"Wire's down," Winthrop said, blinking beneath his green eyeshade. "I'm thinkin' lightning mighta struck up on Murphy Butte east of town and caused rocks to slide and mow down one of my poles. I'll send someone to check on it as soon as the weather clears."

The older man studied the Diamondback sheriff closely. "Say, you not only look soaked to the gills, Des, you look like someone danced a two-step over your grave."

Rainey said, "I just rode out to the Bear-Runner place."

"I heard about that from Calvin. You was supposed to meet Dan Garvey. Who you suppose killed those poor people, Des?"

It was no surprise to Rainey that word of the killings had already traveled around Diamondback. Garvey's hired hand had most likely let the cat out of the bag in the Dragoon Saloon several hours earlier, and it had probably run around Diamondback twice since then.

"I'll tell you later," Rainey said, glancing at the window over his right shoulder. The rain was still coming hard and fast, forming a long waterfall roaring over the depot building's overhang, behind the tied, jittery sorrel. The sheriff cursed under his breath and turned back to Winthrop. "Fetch me when you get the line back up—will you, Edgar?"

"Sure. You wanna leave your message, and I'll send it soon as I can start transmitting again?"

Rainey thought it over. The fewer people who knew about his suspicions the better. He didn't want the killer or killers to know he was on to him or them, and he didn't want to get himself back-shot, either.

On the other hand, he needed to get the message out as quickly as possible. He didn't need to explain the whole nasty business, he just needed help.

"Why not?"

"Here, scribble it on that," Winthrop said, sliding an envelope down the table toward Rainey. He fished a pencil stub out of his pocket and set it atop the envelope.

Rainey leaned down, touched the pencil to his tongue, and scribbled a short note.

"There ya go, Edgar. Send that out just as soon as you can, will you? I'll be in my office."

Winthrop read the pencil-scrawled missive and raised an eyebrow. "The U.S. Marshals, eh? This must be serious, Des."

"Just let me know when you've sent the telegram, Edgar," Rainey said, and turned to the door standing partly open behind him.

"Stay and have a cup of mud with me, Des," the old station agent said, raising his own steaming mug enticingly. "You look like you could use some. I'll splash some busthead in it. Settle your nerves a little."

"Nothin's gonna settle my nerves today, Edgar," Rainey said as he went out, drawing the door closed behind him.

He rode over to one of the two livery barns in town and turned the sorrel over to Ronnie Brown, the son of one of the two brothers who ran the place. Rainey shucked his Winchester from the boot and then strode east along the street toward his office, not bothering to stay under the awning roofs on the street's north side.

He was so soaked that the rain no longer mattered. Also, he wanted to keep a keen eye on both sides of the street for any gunmen who might be lurking there.

Apprehension raked cold fingers across the back of his neck, and he probed the shadows between buildings for a possible bushwhacker—the same man who'd tried to dry-gulch him and Garvey back at the Bear-Runner ranch.

He was relieved when he reached the wooden porch of his small, mud-brick jailhouse and office. He stopped just off the stoop and shuttled a careful gaze up and down the muddy street, and then, seeing nothing suspicious, he mounted the porch. There was no lock on the door, just a steel-and-leather latch outfitted with a six-inch curl of wire.

Rainey looked forward to getting out of his wet clothes and sitting back in his chair with a tall brandy . . .

He threw the door open, stepped inside.

The sheriff stopped suddenly. "What the hell . . . are . . . you doing . . . here . . .?"

His last word was drowned out by a shotgun's thunderous explosion. The blast lifted Des Rainey three feet in the air and threw him back across the porch and into the street, where he landed with a splash in the ankle-deep mud.

Chapter 3

Deputy United States Marshal Custis P. Long, known far and wide to friend and foe as Longarm, checked his army bay down in the shade of the cottonwoods lining the stage road he was following west toward the little ranch supply town of Diamondback, Wyoming Territory, and curveted the mount as it switched its tail at blackflies.

Longarm stared back the way he'd come, at the trail winding up and around the shoulder of a bullet-shaped butte the slopes of which were littered with small boulders and tufts of sage and yucca. No movement on the trail. At least, not for as far back as he could see, which was only about a half a mile.

He saw no dust plumes rising on the other side of the butte, either.

The federal badge toter looked to either side of the bluff, squinting his keen brown eyes beneath the brim of his flat-brimmed, snuff-brown Stetson, tipped over his right eye, cavalry-style, to investigate every nook and cranny, small rocky shelf, and wedge of purple shade, though shade was damn scarce out here except under the occasional tree.

Nothing along his backtrail looked suspicious in the least. In fact, he could see nothing but the facets of the land itself—brush, rocks, a few piñon pines, a scattering of scraggly junipers. At this time of the day, around two, even the jackrabbits were hunkered down in their burrows, out of the hammering sun.

No deer or elk. Damn few birds even, except a couple of warblers scurrying around in the aspens above and behind him.

Damn strange.

For the past half hour, since he'd left the Lone Pine Relay Station of the Wyoming Stage Company, he'd felt that itchy feeling beneath his collar that he felt at only two times. One was just after he'd gotten a haircut and the barber hadn't properly whisked the trimmings away from his neck. The other time was when he was being shadowed—usually by someone with the dreariest of intentions.

It was a feeling the lawman always heeded. Having been a deputy United States marshal in the service of Chief Marshal Billy Vail and Colorado's First District Federal Court in Denver for more years than he cared to count, he'd made his share of enemies. Every year it seemed that either someone he'd once locked up or the family or friends of someone he'd locked up or put away for a long time came gunning for him with the intention of turning him toe-down, sending him off pushing up daisies from the bottom of a deep, black grave.

At the moment, he could see no one on his back-trail. But the prickling under his collar told him that someone was back there, all right.

Sometimes, the best course of action in such a situation was to do as little as possible. If someone were indeed shadowing the lawman with evil intent, there was little reason to keep riding and allow the stalkers to possibly work around him and ambush him. Some-times the best course of action was the least amount of action. He would sit down over there in those trees by that glinting brook, build a fire, boil up some cof-fee, and wait for the fellow or fellows to show himself or themselves.

Maybe they'd even have a cup of coffee together, talk things out in a civilized manner . . .

Longarm gave a wry snort as he reined the big army bay, which he'd requisitioned at the small cavalry out-post near Chugwater, off the trail and headed south through the aspens toward a shallow creek that flashed along the base of a boulder-strewn ridge, rippling and murmuring over rocks.

As the bay moved slowly, stepping around or over fallen branches, its hooves thumping and crunching dead leaves, the lawman cast another cautious look to the east. Beyond the trees and toward the bluff he'd ridden over ten minutes ago, still no movement.

Longarm reined the bay to a halt at the edge of the water lined with tall, green grass, moss, and coffee-colored foam licking at the bank. He stretched his six-foot-three-inch, broad-shouldered frame, outfitted with

the narrow hips and muscular thighs of a veteran
horseman, and then doffed his hat and ran his big,
brown, callused hands through his close-cropped, dark
brown hair. He scratched at his long sideburns and
then ran a sleeve of his tobacco-tweed frock coat
across his sweat-soaked, handlebar mustache.

It had been a long, hot trip out from Denver—
blazes, it had been a hot summer!—and he'd be glad
to get out of the sun for a while. The lawman's face,
burned by many western suns and chewed by many a
cold western wind, was customarily Indian-tan, but
now at the tail end of a long, hot summer, it had been
charred nearly as dark as mahogany. His mustache
and sideburns had been bleached cinnamon, an inter-
esting contrast to the mahogany. They were, in fact,
nearly the exact color as his keen, intelligent eyes that
could flash in jovial good humor and ribald laughter
as easily and as quickly as they could flare in anger
when riled.

Altogether the lawman called Longarm's earthy,
chiseled, darkly handsome looks, accompanied as they
were by a brawny, angular, long-muscled body clad in
a now-dusty three-piece suit with a chocolate brown
string tie, attracted quite a few admiring glances from
the women of the species.

And Longarm had never been a man to brush away
a woman's attentions. In fact, on the long trip out here
by train and horseback he'd entertained himself
remembering the silky, warm, wet lips of Cynthia Larimer. Yes, the heartrendingly beautiful young niece of
Denver's founding father, General Larimer, had
bequeathed to him a French lesson on the grandest

scale the evening before his train departed Union Station for Wyoming.

He would remember the way she'd sucked and tongued and gently nibbled his cock while tickling his balls with her fingertips, holding him teetering on the edge of satisfaction until he'd thought his heart would explode—on his deathbed!

When Longarm had released the bay's latigo and bridle bit, so it could forage and drink at will, he knelt by the stream and dunked his head in the cold water, ridding his mind of the sensation of Cynthia Larimer's lips around his manhood. No use torturing himself.

He donned his hat, rose, and scrounged in the near trees for enough wood to make a coffee fire. While he worked, he kept a close eye on the trail curving just beyond the copse. He kept his ears pricked, as well, but so far he'd heard nothing but the slight breeze, the stream sliding between its broad banks, and the birds fluttering around the branches overhead.

He made coffee, and when the Arbuckle's had come to a boil, he settled the grounds with a little fresh water from his canteen and then filled a fire-blackened tin cup. He was sitting on a log by the fire, sipping the hot brew slowly and staring through the trees toward the trail, when the bay pricked its ears and gave a low nicker deep in its chest. The horse had been facing the stream, nibbling the green grass growing along the bank, but now the mount swung its head around to look toward the trail.

Longarm almost smiled when he, too, began picking up the slow clomps of a rider making his way along the trace.

That old sixth sense of his was as keen as ever.

He remained sitting on the log, leaning forward, elbows on his knees, steaming cup in his gloved hands, listening to the slow thuds growing gradually louder. He stared toward the trail and saw a shadow move. The shadow was shaped like a horse and rider. The rider angled off the trail and into the trees and was making straight for Longarm, slowly.

The horse was a sorrel with a left front stocking and an interrupted stripe down the muzzle. Longarm couldn't tell much about the rider because of the shade cloaking her, but that she was a girl was obvious by the curvy figure clad in a red-and-white checked shirt and faded blue denims with patched knees. Full, round mounds pushed out the shirt and jostled as horse and rider approached through the trees.

When she came out of the trees, the girl stopped the sorrel about ten feet away from Longarm's fire. The lawman's throat swelled and dried as he stared up at her. She was a pretty, suntanned girl with coarse auburn hair hanging straight down past her shoulders from beneath her black Stetson, the chin thong of which dangled across her chest. Her hair was streaked copper by the sun. The girl's eyes were the most striking green Longarm had ever seen.

Her face was expressionless as she stared at Longarm, who canted his head to regard the girl more closely. Seventeen, eighteen, he would say. A tall girl—long-legged and full-busted. Those jade-green eyes were damned off-putting. She wore brush-scarred brown chaps and brown stockmen's boots.

The cat had gotten Longarm's tongue, so the girl

was first to speak, lifting her smoky green gaze to the sun-dappled, cool, refreshing water behind him. "This is my swimmin' hole, mister."

Longarm opened his mouth to tell her that he was sorry for intruding, but then she turned the sorrel around the fire and, clomping past him, turned her head toward him and quirked her mouth corners just slightly, provocatively. Then she turned forward and jogged up along the stream for about fifty yards, her hair bouncing on her shoulders, and stopped.

She swung her long right leg over the cantle of her saddle and leaped fleetly down to the ground, landing and bouncing slightly on the balls of her boots and immediately reaching under the sorrel's belly to release its latigo strap. She slipped the horse's bit from its teeth, dropped the reins, and doffed her black hat.

She tossed the hat on the ground, then reached into one of her saddlebag pouches and pulled out what appeared to be a towel. She tossed the towel over a small pine tree that was not as tall as she was. Glancing at him almost furtively, she stepped behind the tree and lifted her hands to her shirt. Again, she glanced at him, and Longarm turned away discreetly, dipping his nose in his coffee cup and taking a sip, feeling a hard thudding in his chest and a tightening in his crotch.

Christ, was she going to undress right there? Swim right there?

He held his head forward and continued to sip his coffee, making an effort to look nonchalant, but he kept glancing out the left corner of his eye. The girl was moving around over there. He thought he could see clothes being tossed to the ground. When she swung away from the tree, he turned his head toward her, and drew a deep breath.

She was stepping off the bank and into the stream, naked as the day she was born, but a whole lot better filled out.

Christ. She was tall and leggy, all right.

Slender-wasted, shoulders kind of broad in the way of girls who rode a lot get broad-shouldered and long-legged.

He couldn't see her front, but he could see the curve of her left breast under her arm, and it would be one nice handful indeed. She did not turn her head toward him as she walked slowly into the stream, holding her hands out slightly, taking one step at a time, hair dancing across her shoulders.

She walked out beyond the shade of the aspens and cottonwoods, and the sun shone on her. The rich light was like a lens revealing her dimpled, pale, round butt cheeks and another dimple at the small of her back.

The delicate spine curved down from her neck and between her shoulder blades to that beautiful rump any man in his right mind would want to sink his teeth into . . .

When she was about twenty feet out from the bank, she turned to face downstream, toward Longarm, and he turned his head away so sharply that he heard a couple of bones in his neck creak. His heart fluttered. His hands shook, rippling his coffee.

He brought the cup to his lips, sipped. The coffee had grown lukewarm.

He dropped to his knees, used a leather swatch to

lift the pot from the fire, and poured himself another cup. He felt a little sick inside, the way a man will when he's "in season," so to speak. His mannish desire was tempered by his lawman's sense of caution.

A lone girl getting naked out here and swimming around practically before his eyes could very easily be a trap. He kept his ears and eyes skinned, watching and listening for more hoof clomps or the crunch of brush under stealthy feet. Men might be using her to distract him so they could work around him and perforate his hide with hot lead.

A roar sounded in a branch over Longarm's head. His heart leaped in his chest. He dropped his coffee cup on his thigh, and groaned against the burn as he reached across his belly for the Frontier Colt .44 holstered for the cross-draw on his left hip.

He clicked the hammer back while at the same time he lost his balance and fell back on his rump with a shrill curse.

He lifted the Colt's maw, aiming up at the branch, but stayed his trigger finger.

A squirrel hung its head over the aspen branch arcing over him, glaring down at him, flicking its tail and chittering loudly, sounding like an unoiled whipsaw blade.

Longarm depressed the Colt's hammer. "You little bastard," he snapped.

Sitting in the middle of the creek, upstream fifty yards, the girl lounged back on her arms, tipping her head far back on her shoulders, laughing huskily. Her bare breasts jostled as she laughed and idly tapped the heel of one bare foot against the water.

Chapter 4

Longarm's ears warmed as the naked beauty continued to laugh at him.

He curled his lip at the squirrel, who seemed to be laughing at him, too. He looked at the girl again, who kicked her feet in the water and gazed at him over her the swollen mounds of her upthrust breasts. She did nothing to cover herself. In fact, she didn't seem to mind exposing herself to him at all.

A tease, that one. As pretty as she was, she couldn't be too bright, swimming naked out here with a strange man sipping coffee nearby. This was rough country. How did she know he wasn't the sort to walk out there and force himself on her?

Of course, he wasn't that sort. Longarm, good with women, had never had to resort to such crude tactics as rape.

But how did this girl know that?

"You really oughta be more careful, Miss Whoever You Are!" he yelled now as he picked up his coffee cup and gained his feet, anger mixing with his embarrassment. Then, under his breath: "Frolicking naked around a stranger. Who in the hell raised this she-cat—wolves?"

He kept his eyes off of her, still embarrassed, and brushed his glove across his wet pant leg. His thigh was tender from the scalding coffee, though fortunately most of the hot liquid had landed on the ground and not on his leg.

A rumbling sounded. He lifted his head and tipped his hat brim back off his forehead to peer at the sky.

Gray-bellied clouds were closing over the valley. In the far east, lightning forked down from a massive, anvil-shaped storm cloud. The leaves around Longarm rustled as a chill breeze lifted.

Shit, a storm was moving in. He should have kept pushing up the trail to Diamondback, still nearly a day's ride away. Instead, he'd pulled up here to get laughed at by a squirrel and a girl who didn't know any better than to swim naked in front of strangers . . .

His regret at not having kept moving on toward the scene of his next assignment was tempered by the girl, whom he could hear splashing in the stream. She was damn compelling, he had to admit. But then, most naked girls were compelling to any man with blood in his veins.

Not all that sorry that he'd have to wait here until the storm passed, he unsaddled his horse and used his tarpaulin and rope to fashion a lean-to angling off a tree near the fire. Then he scrounged for a couple more armfuls of wood, to get him through the storm, and brewed another pot of coffee.

He continued to keep his senses attuned to his surroundings, always wary of an ambush. He kept them attuned as well to the girl, who, after about twenty minutes of playing like a baby beaver in the flashing water, walked up on the bank, glanced at Longarm coyly, and then stepped behind the pine, which did little to screen her, and began dressing.

Longarm was sitting on his log under the tarpaulin as the first cold raindrops began to slant down out of the leaden sky and the girl walked her horse over to his fire. She stopped just beyond the fire and began unsaddling the mount—moving quickly and sure-handedly, with no wasted motions. This was a girl who'd grown up in the saddle, though judging by how she'd looked naked, she was about as full-grown as they came.

Leaving the horse free to roam, she turned to Longarm, her hair hanging down over one side of her face, lending her a wry, dubious look. One green eye blazed against her pretty, suntanned face.

"Share your fire?"

Longarm hiked a shoulder. His pride kept him from wanting to look too eager, though he would have been crestfallen if the girl had climbed on her horse and ridden away. He'd halfway built the lean-to for her, figuring she'd need a place to get in out of the rain. He hadn't seen any signs of a ranch or a miner's cabin in many miles.

She ducked under the tarpaulin and sat on the log in front of the fire, about three feet to Longarm's right.

He filled his extra cup with the smoking brew and handed it to her, aiming the handle toward her.

"Thanks," she said.

"You always do that?"

"Do what?" she asked as Longarm made himself comfortable on the log once more.

"Swim naked in front of strange men."

"Did you like it?"

Longarm looked at her. Her hair had come down to hide the other half of her face now, exposing the left side and the left blazing green eye that had an almost unsettling depth to it.

"My swimming in front of you?"

Longarm's cheeks and ears warmed. "Young lady, there ain't no man on this earth that don't like to see a pretty girl naked. But that don't mean it's right for said pretty girl to go swimming naked in front of one. Especially way out here in the middle of nowhere. If I'd wanted to take you, there'd have been damn little you could have done about it. And damn few people around to hear your screams for help."

She smiled, her lips shoving a few strands of her hair aside. "How do you know I would have screamed for help? Maybe I would have enjoyed it."

Longarm studied her, incredulous. His pants were growing tighter, pinching his stiffening mast. He looked at the fire, trying to clear his mind of his wild imaginings. "Got a handle?"

"Connie," she said just as a pitch knot popped, sounding like a derringer. She glanced at the cinders climbing skyward. "What's yours?"

"Custis Long. Most folks call me Longarm."

"You're a lawman."

He looked at her again, narrowing one eye. "How did you know that?"

Connie hiked a shoulder. Her left green eye continued blazing into him. So did the right one, from behind the thin screen of her auburn hair. "I guessed it. Something about how strong you look, and the integrity and honesty in your eyes. Even when you're lusting after a girl, imagining rutting around between her legs, sticking your mast in her pussy, you're still of a pure heart. I like that about you, Longarm. I sensed it in you right off. I know good men from bad ones. I've had plenty of experience with the latter, which is why I'm always on the scout for the former. That's why, when I saw you sitting here by my swimming hole, I stayed."

Longarm's voice was thick. "You from around here?"

Connie sipped her coffee and looked out at the rain. "Not going home anytime soon. The arroyos up by my folks' place are gonna be flooded. But doesn't this cool rain feel good?"

She reached forward to let the rain sluicing off the top of the lean-to splash against her hand. She brought the water to her face. She cupped another handful and pressed it to her neck, running the hand down her chest and into her shirt.

Longarm watched her hand. The moisture dribbled down her shirt and pasted it against her breasts. Longarm sipped his coffee and told himself that she was young and a little touched. He wouldn't go near this girl with a ten-foot pole.

This was a bad place for young girls. Too isolated. When their sap started to run, there wasn't much they could do with it. It drove them crazy, like an in-season mare without a stallion to satisfy her body's natural demands. No, this girl was young, and she probably had a pa following from not too far back with a double-barreled shotgun loaded with double-ought buck.

But then those thoughts slithered away like baby snakes in the rain as the girl set her empty cup down on the log, stood, and faced him. She raised her hands and swept her hair back behind her head. The movement caused her shirt to draw back tightly against the twin cones of her breasts, which jutted toward him.

Her eyes blazed down at him as she tied her hair in a loose knot. Feeling jittery and heavy in the belly and loins, Longarm forgot his resolution of only a few seconds ago. He tossed his own cup down and rose and placed his hands on her breasts.

She smiled as she lowered her arms, her hair knotted beguilingly atop her head. A few light freckles were sprayed across the edges of her temples.

She placed her hands on his. They looked like creamy silk against the callused, scarred saddle leather of his thick, brown paws. She caressed his knuckles with her fingertips, dipping her chin toward her chest, smiling down at their hands pressed together atop her breasts.

Longarm pressed the heels of his hands against her shirt, felt her shirt slide across them. Her breasts moved beneath his manipulations, rising and falling as he caressed them. She wore only a thin garment beneath the shirt. He could feel her nipples beneath his thumbs.

The girl lifted her gaze to his and drew a long, deep breath. Color touched the nubs of her cheeks. Slowly, she moved her hands away from his to press them against his chest. She slid them just as slowly down across his belly and over his cartridge belt to his crotch.

She pressed her fingers against his hard-on angling down against his right leg. Pressing gently, she slid her hand from the base of his cock to the bulging head. He drew a sharp breath at the fire that the touch started in his cock, making it feel as if the rock-hard mast were going to tear through his tight, tweed trousers.

She unbuckled his cartridge belt.

Longarm took the belt and set it across the log behind him, not so far gone with lust that he wouldn't keep the .44 near to hand. He still wasn't sure he hadn't walked into a trap, but as he watched the girl expertly unbutton his trousers and slide them down his legs and then reach into the fly of balbriggans, he thought, oh, what a sweet trap it was.

A man wouldn't mind dying in a trap such as this . . .

Her gentle hands reached into his fly. She angled her left hand toward his right thigh, wrapped it around the long, thick gooseneck of his raging hard-on, and closing her upper teeth over her full lower lip and using her right hand to pull his balbriggans out away from his thighs, she gently slid the heavy snake from its hole.

The swollen purple head emerged and rose to angle back against his belly, free at last. It bobbed with each hammering thud of his heart.

She stared down at it. She swallowed.

Her nose only an inch away from the throbbing head, she looked up at him from beneath her brows, lifted her mouth corners, and blinked once, slowly. Her eyes were catlike, glinting in the firelight as the rain washed down around them and drummed loudly on the tarpaulin over their heads.

"That's some axe handle you got there, mister," she said just loudly enough that he could hear her raspy voice above the rain. Still looking up at him, she held his cock by its base with one hand, cupped his heavy balls with her other hand, poked her tongue out of her mouth, and touched the tip to the end to his hard-on.

He gritted his teeth and rocked back on the heels of his boots.

She kept her eyes on him as she held her tongue against the tip of his cock for about ten more excruciating seconds. As though she was well aware of the torturous effect, her cheeks dimpled slightly. Very slowly, she swirled her tongue around the end of his dong until, after he thought his heart would explode in his chest, her cheeks dimpled deeply and then she closed her lips over the entire swollen head.

Her cheeks bulged; her lips compressed against the sides of his member.

Her mouth was hot and wet.

His loins thudded. His heart beat heavily, ramming itself against his sternum.

She slid his mouth down lower on his cock and then pulled it back. She slid it down again and pulled it back, enswathing its entire length with her hot, wet tongue.

Her head bobbed harder and harder in front of him. She slid her mouth off of him and rose until she stood before him. Longarm reached toward her and unbuttoned her blouse while she watched his hands. He tossed the shirt away and lifted her lace-edged chemise up over her head and tossed it over the log.

Her breasts jutted toward him, tan and full. She obviously spent a lot of time naked in the sun, because they were only slightly lighter than the rest of her. They were rich and full, cone-shaped, the pink nipples jutting slightly out to each side.

Longarm lowered his head and nuzzled them, licked them until the nipples stood out like April cottonwood buds about to burst. The girl groaned and sandwiched his head in her hands, grinding his face against her bosoms until she stepped back abruptly and kicked out of her boots.

Longarm kicked out of his low-heeled Cavalry stovepipes. He shrugged out of his coat, jerked the knot free of his string tie, and tossed the tie on the log with the coat.

The girl was faster than he at getting undressed. By the time he'd finally kicked free of his right balbriggan leg and stood naked by the fire, his cock standing up like a pump handle before him, the girl was already naked and had spread her clothes out on the ground by the fire.

She lay down quickly at his feet, spread her legs, and reached toward him, groaning, the folds of her snatch peeling back from the silky hair at her crotch and opening like a mouth, its tiny pink tongue extended.

Longarm took a cursory glance around to make sure no one was drawing a bead on him, and then dropped to his knees. He leaned forward between Connie's knees, and as she raised her legs high, opening herself wider for him, she grunted and groaned and reached down to grab his cock. She ground it against her pussy until she'd worked up a good lather, and then she slid the bulging head inside her.

"Oh, God!" she said, throwing her head back and hardening her jaws, squinting up at the tarpaulin roof as the rain continued to hammer it. "Oh, fuck me! Damn you, fuck me!"

Propped on his outstretched arms and his toes, Longarm slowly slid his cock into the girl's hot, sopping snatch. She groaned and cursed like an Irish sailor, and when he'd gotten all of his shaft that he could deep inside her, she ground her heels against his rump, wrapped her arms around his neck, and drew him even deeper.

He drew his butt up and down, sliding in and out of her, in and out, gradually building to a faster and faster rhythm until he was pistoning like a locomotive's drive shaft, and working up a hot sweat as he toiled. He could feel the girl's sweat ooze beneath him as their hips and bellies slapped together loudly, wildly.

When he came, it was like the rain hammering down around him and on the lean-to. He groaned and shuddered, propped on his arms and toes, seed jetting deep into the dark, boiling depths of her womb. She'd turned her head to one side and squealed as she bit down hard on the knuckles of her right hand.

As he and Connie finished together, she drew a

ragged breath. She turned to him, her eyes smoky and slightly crossed. She sandwiched his head in her hands and pressed her mouth to his. She kissed him passionately, deeply, grinding her breasts and hips against him as though terrified that now that he'd spent himself he'd leave her.

He didn't leave her. He merely rolled to one side and tossed another log onto the fire, building the flames back up again, for the damp air owned a definite chill. Then he glanced outside the tarpaulin. The rain had relented slightly but was still coming down.

Neither Longarm nor the girl was going anywhere anytime soon.

He rolled toward her and she enfolded him in her arms and kissed her, liking the way her young, tender lips felt against his. Soon, he'd become hard again, and she gave a sexy little titter and scuttled down beneath him until his cock was lying up snug in the valley between her breasts.

"Fuck my titties," she said in a voice pinched with passion. It sounded like a little girl's voice, enflaming him even more.

As she squeezed her full breasts together around his cock, he slid the shaft up and down, up and down, until he'd brought himself to the edge of his passion once more. He tumbled on over the edge, his seed spurting against the underside of Connie's chin. She lowered her chin and he finished with the last streams spitting across her lips, which she lapped clean with her tongue.

They slept spooned together after that, him holding her from behind. He'd drawn his bedroll over them both. Distantly, he heard the pitter-patter of the lessening storm on the ground and on the tarpaulin. The thunder rumbled into the distance.

The fire kept him and the girl warm. The piney smell of the wood smoke was a nice complement to the cool breeze and the rain.

When he woke sometime later, she was gone. It was as though she'd never been there at all.

Chapter 5

Longarm yawned and fisted sleep from his eyes.

He looked around for signs of Connie. The strange feeling that he'd merely dreamed her lingered.

The surreal feeling that clung to him like sticky cobwebs did nothing to help the matter. He'd probably slept only a couple of hours, but as groggy as he remained, he felt as though he'd slept as long as Rip Van Winkle. The fire had nearly died, only a few flames licking up from one charred log that had not totally burned to gray ashes.

The rain had stopped. It was dusk. Moisture dripped from the tarpaulin and from the trees around it.

All around him the dripping forest was quiet save for the distant, intermittent hooting of an owl.

It was a peaceful sound but also an eerie sound at this time of the day, in a strange place on the lee side of a storm at dusk. The trees were dark against the dark gray sky. The stream was charcoal gray, white where it bubbled over rocks.

Sitting up with the blanket draped over his shoulders, Longarm looked around. He could see no sign of Connie. No bare footprint in the dirt around the fire. The cup she'd drank from was no longer where he remembered that she'd dropped it. And he had absolutely no memory of her leaving.

By necessity, Longarm was a light sleeper. When the girl awoke, he should have felt her move out from under his arms and heard her stirring. His ears were keen. But he had no memory of feeling or hearing anything.

True, it had been a long trip and he'd given Connie quite a workout, but he hadn't been so exhausted and slept so deeply that he wouldn't have awakened when a girl left his arms.

Puzzling.

He shook his head, blinked, raked a hand down his face. She'd been here, he told himself. She hadn't been a dream. He remembered her in detail—every beautiful inch of her. A man didn't dream in such detail as that. Besides . . .

He lowered a hand to his cock. It felt tacky, the way it usually did after he'd coupled. It was also a little chafed.

Of course, a wet dream could explain the residue on his dong. And he could have chafed the member by grinding it against the ground while dreaming he'd been fucking an auburn-haired, green-eyed forest sprite.

Doubtful.

Oh, well. If she'd been a dream, then she'd been one

hell of a dream. He couldn't wait to go back to sleep and have the same dream again . . .

He looked around once more, skeptically. The bay stared back at him from thirty yards downstream, and then went back to gazing off over the water. The horse was soaked from the rain but otherwise seemed no worse for the storm.

Longarm gained his feet, shed the blanket, and walked naked to the stream's edge. He stepped into the water, sucking a sharp breath against the cold sliding up his legs. After a quick bath, he returned to the camp, dressed, and then built up the fire again, and went to work warming up the leftover beans and rabbit he'd had for the previous night's supper.

While the food warmed on the hot coals, he made coffee and then sat back and drank a cup spiced with his beloved Maryland rye. He smoked one of his three-for-a-nickel cheroots and stared out over the creek, still wondering despite himself if he'd actually made love to the girl named Connie, or if she'd merely been a dream.

For some damned crazy reason, he just couldn't be sure!

When he'd eaten and had cleaned his cooking utensils in the stream, he vowed to stop thinking about the rendezvous. He had bigger fish to fry—namely, his current assignment, which had him riding up to the town of Diamondback on the eastern edge of the Wind River Range. Apparently, a lawman friend of Billy Vail's had requested help from the chief marshal's office, and Billy had sent his seniormost deputy, Longarm himself.

That, too, was strange. Not in the same way his experience or non-experience with the girl had been strange, but strange in the fact that the town sheriff of Diamondback, Des Rainey, had sent such a cryptic note, which read only:

> *Billy,*
>
> *If you can spare a man, I could use some help up here. Can't go into detail. Rest assured, it's serious.*
>
> *Thanks, Des Rainey.*

Longarm's boss, Chief Marshal Billy Vail, had sent a note back asking Rainey to go into at least a little more detail, but the message had gone unanswered. In the two weeks since Rainey had sent the note, Billy had not heard another word from the man, whom he had worked with more than twenty years ago, when they'd both ridden for the Texas Rangers.

It was Longarm's job to find out what in the hell was going on up at Diamondback and to render assistance where needed. This was not officially a federal matter, but deputy U.S. marshals were often sent to the aid of local lawmen who called for it. Especially to the aid of local lawmen who were close friends of chief marshals.

Darkness fell down like a thick, black glove over the valley. The sky cleared and the stars shimmered like sequins in the treetops.

Longarm built up his fire against the post-storm

chill, and, gently sliding the puzzle of the girl from his mind one more time—hopefully for the last time—he evacuated his bladder into the stream and then rolled up in his blankets by the fire.

It took a while, but he finally went to sleep, and woke fairly well rested the next morning at dawn. He was saddled and mounted and back on the trail after a quick cup of coffee and three or four bites of jerky. He wasn't sure exactly where he was on the government survey map he'd picked up at the outpost near Chugwater, but he thought he still had a good half a day's ride ahead of him.

Continuing west through the valley, by midmorning he crossed a low divide. Riding down the other side, he shucked his brown frock coat and wrapped it over his bedroll. The sun was heating up. Sweat was popping out on his forehead and dripping down his cheeks and into his shirt. He rolled his sleeves up his forearms and tipped his hat brim low as the sun continued to climb and grow brassier and hotter.

Longarm followed the next broad, high-desert valley for another two-and-a-half hours, stopping frequently to rest and water his horse and to give his own backside a breather.

Ahead, the Wind Rivers rose, dark and brooding against the western sky. To the north jutted the Bighorns. To the south were the Laramies. This was a big, mountainous country relieved by broad valleys and scored by deep canyons, with massive mesas jutting for as far as the eye could see.

A man riding through such terrain felt no larger or more significant than a spider.

Somewhere near the base of the Wind Rivers was the town Longarm was heading for, though he wasn't able to see Diamondback until he was a mile away from it. Looking little larger from that distance than a postage stamp, the settlement was lost on the floor of a bowl-shaped valley hemmed in on all sides by forbiddingly rugged peaks. It sprawled atop a low bluff, some of its outlying dwellings spilling down the bluff's sides.

Diamondback looked little different from most isolated ranch supply towns Longarm had seen in the past. The trail he was on became the town's main drag, cleaving it in two from east to west. There appeared to be about a two-hundred-yard section of false-fronted business buildings constructed of wood or adobe brick. None looked significant enough to withstand the brutal winds known to howl through this rugged country, but apparently they were.

As beaten and weathered as they appeared, they'd been standing for a good dozen years or so.

Outlying shanties and stock pens dropped back on both sides of the trail as Longarm entered Diamondback. On his left was a building whose large shingle identified it as the WYOMING STAGE COMPANY with smaller signs announcing TELEGRAPHER and U.S. MAIL. It was a low-slung, mud-brick structure with a brush-roofed front veranda.

A man stood atop the veranda, leaning up against a roof support post at the top of the steps, arms crossed on his chest. He was an old, gray-bearded gent wearing a green eyeshade, a blue wool vest with gold buttons, and sleeve garters.

Longarm's bay clomped along the main street, approaching the front of the stage line's local depot building, its hooves lifting a fine, powdery dust that glowed like copper in the harsh sunshine. Scowling suspiciously at the stranger astraddle the bay, the old man in the green eyeshade lowered his arms and stepped slowly back from the porch post. He kept his scowling gaze on Longarm as he edged back and over toward the door propped open behind him, as though hoping he hadn't been noticed.

Longarm pinched his hat brim in a friendly greeting at the oddly behaving old-timer, who slipped through the dark doorway behind him to disappear into the dingy bowels of the depot building. Longarm stared, frowning, at the dark open door.

Apparently, someone in Diamondback wasn't all that happy to see him. It wasn't all that uncommon for folks to shy away from lawmen. Such leeriness was natural even in folks who weren't guilty of any crimes. Longarm wasn't wearing his badge, for nothing made a better target in open country, but he supposed his attire—he obviously wasn't a cowhand—and the .44 holstered for the cross-draw on his left hip, might have given him away.

He shrugged off the depot agent's reaction and continued along the street. There wasn't much traffic. It was probably too hot for most folks to be out. Longarm could see at least three saloons, and a few horses had been tied to the hitchracks fronting each.

As he passed the Dragoon Saloon on his right, a

man inside stepped up to look over the batwings, a
beer held in one hand. Hatless, he was a crude-looking
hombre, with stringy hair and a thick, brushy, sand-
colored mustache hiding his mouth. He glanced behind
him, canted his head toward Longarm, and the lawman saw another man sidle up to the first. He was
taller, and he, too, stared over the batwings and into
the street at the newcomer.

Longarm turned his head forward. He saw the shingle for the sheriff's office and jail ahead and on his
right, around a slight bend in the street. Across from
the jailhouse, on Longarm's left, was a three-story hotel
of pink brick called the Diamondback Hotel. Just up
the same side of the street were a law office and a bank.

Between the two buildings was an alley, and in the
mouth of the alley were two well-dressed men—one
tall and slender; the other, short and wiry, with pewter
hair and matching mustache. They were standing close
together talking, but as Longarm passed them the
taller man nudged the shorter man, and they both
turned to watch Longarm angle over toward the sheriff's office.

Something told Longarm that one of the well-
dressed gents was the lawyer; the other, the banker.

As he pulled the bay to a halt in front of the sheriff's office—a small, mud-brick affair with a woven-
brush roof, set behind a narrow wooden stoop, he
glimpsed movement in a third-story hotel window. He
narrowed his eyes to scrutinize the window more
closely. It was hard to tell in the harsh, midday light,
but he thought he saw a woman in a red dress look out

at him before drawing her head back quickly behind a white lace curtain.

Longarm swung down from the bay's back. He glanced again toward the alley in which the well-dressed gents were still standing, staring toward him. Under his return gaze, they both jerked slightly as though startled, and turned to each other. They both muttered a few words and then parted, the shorter man walking into the bank, the taller man disappearing into the law office.

Longarm glanced at the third-story hotel window in which he'd seen what he thought was a pretty woman in a red dress. She was no longer there.

He cleared his throat dubiously. It was still best to not make too much of the reactions his presence had evoked. This was a remote town, and strangers of any stripe were often met with suspicion.

The rangy lawman threw his reins over the lone, weather-silvered pine pole that served as a hitchrack, walked up onto the jailhouse's front porch, tapped once on the door, and tripped the steel and leather latch. He pushed the door open and squinted into the dense velvety shadows.

The man who'd been sitting in front a rolltop desk on his left jerked his head up so quickly from where it had been tipped toward his chest that he spilled the coffee he'd been holding in one hand and dropped the thin book with a yellow pasteboard cover that he'd been holding in the other hand.

The man jerked his red face toward Longarm, scowling. "What the . . . ?" His right hand slid toward the pearl-gripped revolver holstered low on his right thigh clad in striped broadcloth.

His dark brown eyes glinted angrily, his nostrils flared, and his black mustache twitched. "Just what in the fuck do you think you're doin', asshole, bargin' in here like you own the damn place!"

Longarm watched the man's right hand close over the pearl grips of his holstered Peacemaker. "If you draw that hogleg, sonny, you best be right good with it."

He paused as the man continued to glare at him.

"And right sure that that's what you want to do," Longarm added, arching his brows and splaying his right hand on his belly, near his own Colt .44.

Chapter 6

The man sitting in the chair with his hands on the pearl grips of his Peacemaker studied Longarm skeptically.

Hesitation touched his mud-black eyes. A slight flush rose in his cheeks, which were covered with a two- or three-day growth of scraggly black beard stubble, over greasy, large-pored skin that didn't take the sun well. He had a scar on the nub of his left cheek, just above the beard. A sheriff's badge was pinned to his shabby wool vest.

"Who the fuck are you?" he barked, keeping his hand on his pistol.

"Deputy U.S. Marshal Custis P. Long. I'm here to see Sheriff Des Rainey. Who are you? Deputy?" Longarm knew the man before him wasn't Rainey. Billy Vail had told him that his old friend was six feet or thereabouts.

The man's demeanor changed abruptly. Drastically. The scar on his left cheek twitched and the color

drained out of his face. He released the handle of his
S&W and let his gaze flick around like two bugs trying to find their way through a window.

"No, no," he said, glancing sheepishly at the badge
on his vest. "The sheriff is . . . uh . . . he's out of town."

"Where?"

"Where?" Now he looked peeved. "Well, I ain't sure
that's any of your damn business." He rose from his
chair and idly brushed at the coffee that had sprayed
across his shirt and vest. His belligerence was back.
Standing a good six inches shorter than Longarm,
he had to look up at him. "What do you want with
him, anyway? And how do I know you're who you say
you are?"

"You get a lot of men coming here professing to be
deputy United States marshals, do you, mister?"

The man didn't seem to know how to answer that.
He just continued to rake his hand slowly across the
coffee stain on his vest and peer up skeptically at
Longarm.

"Well, do you?" Longarm said. He did not like this
man at all. That he was a son of a bitch was obvious
by his demeanor and by the way he dressed and by the
pearl-gripped pistol he carried in his holster. The gun
didn't fit him—it was too pretty for him—but he
wished it did.

"No, I don't reckon," the man said, his eyes working around in their sockets again, gravitating toward
a whiskey bottle on the cluttered desk before him. "I'm
just sayin' . . . you know . . . a fella can't be too careful who he talks to. Who he tells where the sheriff's
at . . . that's all . . ."

He stared at the bottle.

"Who are you?" Longarm said, removing his hand from his own gun and hooking his thumbs behind his cartridge belt.

"Melvin Little. I'm fillin' in, you might say." Little glanced at the badge again, as if he suddenly wished it weren't there.

"And where's Sheriff Rainey?"

"Hell if I know," Little said, jerking his head toward the door. "All I know is I'm replacin' him here for now. Orders of the town council. Why don't you ask them where he went?"

Longarm wasn't satisfied with the answer in the least. He doubted this unshaven, unwashed tinhorn with the expensive gun and the badge he still needed to grow into could tell the truth if his life depended on it.

"You must have some idea."

Little looked around the room as though for an answer. He was getting even more riled, more impatient. "Hell, I don't know. North!" He threw his arm at the door. "That's where he headed. North. There was some beef collared up around Beulah Springs and he rode up there to check it out!"

Longarm kept his gaze hard and commanding as he stared down at the man shifting around uncomfortably before him. "You sure about that?" He pitched his voice with threat.

"Sure enough!"

"Where exactly? Who's ranch? I'll ride out and meet him."

"I don't know. They didn't tell me who's ranch he rode out to!"

"Who's 'they'?"

"The town council."

Longarm was even more skeptical, and he was also growing more and more uneasy. "Why wouldn't Rainey have told you himself? You are his deputy, aren't you?"

"No, I ain't his deputy, big man. I'm just sittin' in for him."

"The town council gave you the job?"

"That's right."

"Who's on the town council?"

Little blinked up at Longarm, hesitating. "Doc Baker, Charlie Mulligan, and Alexander Richmond."

Towns as small as Diamondback often had very small town councils, which weren't really councils at all, but three mucky-mucks who got together to call the shots. "Where can I find these men?"

"What the hell you wanna bother them for? Listen, you got no call to come barging in here stirrin' up trouble."

"I didn't know I was stirrin' up trouble," Longarm said, raising his voice. "I was just asking where I'd find Sheriff Rainey, and you got all riled over that. Would you mind telling me why?"

"I ain't riled. You're the one who's riled!"

Longarm looked down. The man's right hand was once again closed over the pearl grips of his .45. Longarm said nothing. Little followed his gaze to his own hand. He released the pistol, looking sheepish.

He slacked down in his chair, turned toward the desk as though he were about to get back to work, and tossed his hand at the door. "Go on, get outta here! I don't got time to listen to a bunch of federal blarney! Go on an' leave me alone. I don't get paid near enough to put up with this shit."

Longarm gave a wry chuff as he stared down at Little, obviously a small-time gunslinger whom the councilmen had pinned a badge to. They probably hadn't been able to find anybody else. The question was, why had they needed to?

"All right. I'll leave . . . for now. But I'll be back, Mr. Little. You can count on that."

Longarm backed toward the door. He wouldn't put it past the nervous, angry Little to shoot him between his shoulder blades. Little turned his wicked, deceitful gaze on him once more. "Rainey called you in?"

Longarm stopped at the door. "That's right. You know why?"

Little turned his head toward the desk. His eyes were as scared as they were nervous and angry. He didn't say anything, so Longarm walked out across the narrow porch and down the steps to the street.

Frustrated, he looked around. He thought he saw a shadow move quickly away from a window in the bank. He looked up at the Diamondback Hotel and thought he saw a shadow move in the same window in which he'd seen the pretty woman looking out at him before.

He rolled it through his mind.

The sheriff calls on his chief marshal friend for help, but when help arrives, said help finds a nervous, belligerent little man who fancies himself a gunfighter in the sheriff's position. In the sheriff's own chair, in fact. And none of the little man's stories about where

Longarm could find the sheriff made any sense. Nor
did they sound believable.

In fact, they sounded fishy as hell.

Now the strange looks that Longarm had been
greeted with when pulling into town seemed all the
more suspicious and ominous, as well.

He looked up and down the street, pondering his
next course of action. He'd just decided to start beating the bushes for the three-man town council when
he heard the jailhouse door open behind him. He
glanced over his shoulder to see Little staring out the
partly open door.

He was wearing a funnel-brimmed black hat with
a snakeskin band. He hadn't been wearing the hat a
minute ago. Apparently, he was on his way out. Heading where?

The man's left nostril flared, and he slammed the
door.

Longarm reconsidered his notion of seeking out the
town council. It might be best to let Little start spreading the word of what Longarm was in town for. Nervous
rats always made more noise than contented ones. Of
course, that noise might come in the form of gunfire,
but that was a risk Longarm was willing to take, since
it was more or less his job to take it.

He'd kill some time locating a livery barn and sta-
bling his horse. He'd bet that by the time his tack hit
the saddle tree and the bay had started munching oats,
word of Longarm's discussion, if you could call it that,
with Melvin Little would be ripping through the town
like flames fed by a hot western wind.

He slipped his reins from the hitchrack, swung onto

the bay's back, and reined the horse west along the street, which suddenly seemed even quieter than when Longarm had first ridden into town. He continued riding until, about halfway between the jailhouse and the west end of town, he spied a livery barn sitting on a northern cross street.

As he approached, he saw that a large painted sign stretching over the barn's second story, above the hayloft doors, announced CASCADE LIVERY AND FEED, BROWN BROS., PROP. A slender young man in dusty, hay-flecked trousers and a white shirt was sitting on a chair outside the barn's open doors, whittling what appeared to be a horse out of a chunk of pine, and not too handily.

Appearing around seventeen or eighteen, the long-limbed, gangly lad had long red hair and a pimply, pale complexion. He watched Longarm approach and then set the stick and his barlow knife aside and rose from his old kitchen chair, brushing shavings from his pants.

"Help you, mister?" he said, squinting and wincing against the harsh midday light.

"You sure can, son," Longarm said, trying to sound jovial. "You can house this old cayuse for me. I tell you—I'll be plenty happy to get us both out of the sun. Damn, it's hot!"

"It shore is!"

"Tell me—where's the best place to wet one's whistle around here?" Longarm said, handing the kid his reins.

"Ah, I wouldn't know." The kid took the reins and poked his shabby hat back off his forehead as he gazed toward the main street. "My folks don't let me drink nothin' but milk an' sarsaparilla, but most of the fellas seem to like the Dragoon best."

"That's the busiest, usually?"

"Yeah, usually, but you won't have no trouble gettin' a drink in there now. On Saturday night is when you'd best get there first thing, I hear." The kid looked around cautiously, as though to make sure no one else was in earshot, and then leaned toward Longarm, closing one eye deviously. "Old Walter Tattermyer's got him some girls that I hear . . . well, they'll do about anything a man wants . . . if you get my drift, mister."

The kid snickered, showing his long, white horse teeth.

"No, shit?" Longarm said. "You mean, even . . . ?"

"Yep, that's what I hear. For only two dollars, too! Me—I'm thinkin' about savin' up and then goin' in the back way one of these nights, so word don't get around." The boy frowned suddenly and looked up at Longarm skeptically. "Say, you wouldn't tell no one what I just said, would you, mister? If my ma ever found out, she'd crack me over the head with her broom handle!"

"Your secret's safe with me." Longarm laughed and stuck out his hand. "I'm Custis Long, but you can call me Longarm."

"I'm Ronnie Brown," the boy said, jerking his chin toward the big sign nailed to the barn. "My Pa and his brother Wilfred own this place, but I'm about the only one who works here. I bust my butt feedin' horses and shovelin' shit and polishing the rental buggies, and all they do is fish or play horseshoes."

Quickly, so as to try and catch the kid off guard,

Longarm said, "Say, Ronnie, you wouldn't happen to know where my old friend Des Rainey is, would you? I rode all the way out here from Denver, and he doesn't seem to be in his office."

The kid studied him closely, apprehensively. "You . . . uh . . . mean . . . the sheriff?"

"That's right. Any idea where I might find him?"

Along with bartenders and whores, livery boys were often the best sources of information, as men's lives tended to rotate around drink, sex, and horses. Longarm hated to put the lad on the spot, but he had a feeling it might very well be for a higher cause—namely, the well-being of Des Rainey.

"Sheriff Rainey?"

"That's right, Ronnie—Sheriff Rainey. I bet he stabled his horse with you, didn't he? If he'd lit out anywhere, he'd have picked up his horse here, maybe mentioned where he was going."

Ronnie looked around owlishly. "I don't know what you're talkin' about, mister. If . . . if Sheriff Rainey ain't in his office, I sure as hell don't know where he is. Now, why don't you leave me alone to tend your horse or you can just tend him yourself!"

Ronnie glared at Longarm, red-faced with anger and fear. His eyes were rheumy, as though he were near tears. Longarm wasn't going to get any more out of the boy than he had out of Little.

Someone had put the fear of God in him.

Longarm raised his hands. "All right, boy. All right."

The kid turned away and began leading the bay into the barn.

"Hold on," Longarm said, and walked over and slid his Winchester '73 from the saddle scabbard. When he'd draped his saddlebags over his shoulder, Ronnie looked away from him quickly and continued leading the bay into the barn.

Longarm stared after him, scowling. Finally, he hiked the saddlebags higher on his shoulder, set his rifle on the opposite shoulder, reached into his shirt pocket, and pulled out a three-for-a-nickel cheroot. When he was this frustrated, he liked to chew some of it out on a smoke.

Swinging around and striding toward the main street, he fired a match on his thumbnail and touched the flame to the cheroot. When he had the cigar burning to his satisfaction, he tossed the match into the dirt. He smoked as he walked. The dirt was so hot beneath his boots that he felt as though he were walking through coals.

But as hot as the sun was, a cold fist had hold of his guts. Something told him that fist was likely to squeeze all the harder before it finally let go.

Chapter 7

The Dragoon Saloon sat kitty-corner across the street from the jailhouse, about three buildings east of the pink brick hotel.

Longarm stepped onto the boardwalk out front of the place and under the saloon's front awning, relieved to finally have the sun off his head. Hearing a loud buzz of commotion emanating from inside, he slowed his pace as he headed for the batwings. He stopped. The buzz continued. The men inside seemed to have a lot to talk about.

Their tone was owly, befuddled, angry.

Longarm felt a self-satisfied smile quirk his mouth corners around the burning cheroot in his teeth. That wildfire he'd set earlier had indeed spread as far as the Dragoon Saloon, at least.

He swung through the batwings and stopped just inside, letting the doors swing manically behind him before they scraped to an abrupt stop. That seemed to

be the signal for everyone in the long, heavily shadowed room to swing a head toward him.

The conversation stopped as abruptly as the doors
had closed.

Five men stood with their backs to the bar. A half
dozen or so others sat at three separate tables to the
left of the bar. The men at the bar had been joining the
conversation—a single conversation, it seemed—of
the men sitting at the tables.

One of those men was none other than Melvin Little
himself. He sat perched on a chair back, feet on the
chair, leaning forward on his knees, a sheepish look
on his face. His sheriff's badge glinted in the light
from the windows. He turned his head slowly away
from Longarm, like a cowed dog, and looked down at
the table before him.

Two big men sat at his table, both watching Longarm with grim, belligerent looks on their faces—one
bearded, the other with only a mustache. Both men
wore dusters, and they were heavily armed. The one
with only the mustache nodded his head slightly at the
newcomer and stretched his lips back from his teeth
in a menacing grin.

Longarm walked over to the bar, set his rifle and
saddlebags on the bartop to his right, and looked at the
bartender—a short, thick, muscular man with a bull
chest and Indian and Mexican features. His broad,
clean-shaven face looked as though it had been used by
a blacksmith's apprentice to practice hammering on. He
regarded Longarm blankly, thick, chapped lips pursed.

"I'd like a beer and a shot of Maryland rye," Longarm said.

"Don't got none of that stuff," said the barman.

"The beer or the rye?"

The thick bartender just looked at him.

Longarm smiled and said, "All right, how about a beer and whatever kind of rye you got?"

Keeping his dark eyes on Longarm, the thick man grabbed a beer schooner from a pyramid atop the bar and a shot glass from another pyramid near the schooners. He splashed whiskey into the shot glass, filled the schooner from a spigot, and set both on the bar in front of Longarm.

The room had fallen so quiet that the bartender's movements and even his heavy, raspy breathing sounded inordinately loud.

Outside, a hot wind blew. Dust ticked against the front of the place and billowed across the scarred puncheon floor beneath the batwings. A horseback rider passed, hooves thumping slowly, tack squawking, the horse's bridle rattling when the mount shook its head.

The barman said, "Nickel for the beer. Twelve cents for the whiskey."

Longarm reached into his trouser pocket, pulled out some gold and silver, and tossed three coins onto the bar top. They rattled around until the bartender slapped his hand down hard on top of them and then scraped them off the bar and into a coin box.

Longarm took a long pull from the beer. It was warm and sudsy and the yeast tickled his throat, but it cut the trail dust. He set the beer down. He'd lowered the level a good four inches. He raised it an inch by pouring the whiskey into the beer, causing it to foam.

Sometimes the venomous tangleleg in these backwater settlements was best diluted by beer.

Longarm sipped the drink, glancing into the mirror behind the bartender, who had gotten busy mixing flour and some other things into a mixing bowl to Longarm's left. The bull-chested man kept glancing owlishly at the stranger as Longarm kept an eye on the back-bar mirror, knowing that something would happen sooner or later.

He wasn't sure what that would be, but judging by the pregnant, ominous silence and the dead stares being cast his way, he wouldn't doubt if one or more of the Dragoon Saloon's clientele were to try to back-shoot him.

At least, he had to be ready for it.

He'd let them make their move, if one was forthcoming. And then maybe he could get down to the business of finding out what had happened to Sheriff Des Rainey.

He didn't have to wait long. He'd taken one more sip of the whiskey-spiced beer and was sucking the foam from his mustache, when he saw one of the two, big, nasty-looking hombres—the bearded one—rise from his chair. The chair made a loud, raucous sound as the man slid it back from the table. He straightened like a bull in a pasture finding that one of the neighbor's bulls had wandered into his territory.

He'd no sooner stood than the other big-ugly, with the mustache, rose from his own chair, making even more noise than the first one.

The bearded one walked around the table that he and the other big man and Melvin Little had been sitting at, a half a glass of frothy beer in his fist. He had a big belly pushing out his striped shirt. Sweat was a giant dark tongue staining his shirt from his neck to his bulging belly.

As the man approached, kicking out his legs like he was warming up for a dance, his stench wafted against Longarm, who winced against the sour, rancid odor of a man who hadn't bathed in a month of Sundays and likely slept with wolves in a too-small burrow. He wore two pistols on his hips, as did the other man, with the mustache, who also had a shotgun slung over his shoulder by a thick leather lanyard. An old Spencer .56 carbine leaned against the table he'd left.

Altogether, the two were outfitted well enough to be shotgun messengers or bodyguards of a sort.

The bearded man took a too-casual sip of his beer, smacked his lips, and said to Longarm's left shoulder, "Hey, you."

Longarm, leaning forward against the bar, had been watching the men in the mirror. Now he looked at the bearded gent over his left shoulder. "Me?"

"Yeah, you." This from the mustached man, who had coal-black hair and gray eyes and was a little shorter and broader than the bearded gent. He stood just behind and to one side of his friend.

Longarm took another sip of his drink and straightened, sucking the foam from his mustache. "Okay, let's have it," he said in a droll, patient tone. He'd been in the situation of the unwanted stranger so many times before that it was beginning to be old hat.

"We heard from Melvin yonder that you come into town askin' a bunch of questions that ain't none of your business," the bearded man said.

"Yeah, that's what Melvin said," said the mustached man, jutting his dimpled chin at Longarm. He appeared to have lice, tiny miniature rice, clinging to his hair ends. Longarm wasn't sure which man smelled worse but altogether they were making him feel sick to his stomach.

Both pairs of eyes staring at him were glassy from drink.

"I'm sorry, friends," Longarm said amiably, "but I didn't do any such thing."

"What?" said the mustached man. "You callin' Melvin a liar?"

"No, not all. I'm calling him a tinhorned, limp-dicked peckerwood, and I'm calling you two the same. Not only that, but you both stink like a sow giving birth, and you're ugly as last year's sin. Now, unless you can answer the question I posed to Melvin, kindly retreat from my air space so I can take another breath without vomiting my guts out on the floor."

Both men stared at Longarm dumbly, as though neither could quite believe his ears. They looked as though they'd both been backhanded.

Finally, the bearded man, nearest Longarm, bunched his jaws and said, "Friend, I don't care if you're a federal badge toter or not. You just made the wrong pair of enemies, an' you're about to pay dearly for it!"

He hadn't finished that last before he swung his beer schooner back toward his shoulder and then launched it toward Longarm's head. Longarm had seen that coming two weeks ago. He merely stepped into it, raised his left arm, deflecting it, and got a little beer splashed across his back as he smashed his right fist hard against his attacker's bearded jaw.

He smashed him twice more before the big man knew what was happening.

The bearded man stumbled backward, eyes rolling back in his head, as his partner launched himself at Longarm, throwing his arms around the lawman as though he were just so happy to see him he couldn't contain himself.

"You dirty dog—you're gonna die, lawman!" he bellowed as he tried to toss Longarm to the floor.

It didn't work. Longarm was five inches taller than the mustached gent.

Longarm head-butted the man, and when the man released his hold on him, Longarm smashed him once with a right cross and once with a left uppercut. He stepped on the man's right boot to hold him in place and then let him have two more of the same before the mustached gent, nose exploding like a ripe tomato, stumbled backward and onto a table, sending the table's three occupants quickly grabbing their drinks and scattering in all directions.

The table tipped over and the mustached gent and the table hit the floor with a loud, thundering bang! The mustached gent bellowed like a poleaxed bull.

"Son of a bitch!" raged the bearded gent, heaving himself to his feet and hurling himself at Longarm from six feet away.

His intention apparently was to bull into Longarm and pin him against the bar. Longarm had seen that one taking shape a month ago.

He merely stepped to one side, spreading his boots

wide and grabbing the back of the big, bearded man's shirt collar and heaving him in the same direction he'd been headed.

Only harder.

He slammed the man's head against the edge of the bar with a resounding, cracking thump.

When he released the man's collar, the bearded gent dropped straight to the floor like a fifty-pound sack of seed corn hurled from a second-story loading door.

The mustached man was cursing and snarling like a wounded wolf on the floor, trying to pull his shotgun around in front of him. When he finally did so, aiming the double-bored popper at Longarm, the federal lawman stepped toward the man, swinging his right foot up savagely. The square toe of his cavalry boot connected soundly with the underside of the barrel as well as the mustached gent's left hand just as the man triggered the weapon.

Ka-booommmm!

Orange flames and gray smoke knifed at the ceiling. The double-ought buck punched a deep gouge out of the wainscoting, causing slivers and dust to rain. A floor above the saloon, a girl screamed shrilly, "Stop it! Oh, god, stop it!"

Longarm stepped back and looked from the bearded man, who lay unconscious at the base of the bar, head resting on his arms, to the mustached man, who leaned back on his elbows on the floor, his face swollen and bleeding, one bloody upper tooth embedded in his thick lower lip.

Longarm shrugged. "You heard the girl. I'm game if you are. You boys had enough?"

He toed the bearded gent's bulging belly. "Looks like he has." He relieved the unconscious man of his weapons, tossing both pistols across the room, and then he did the same to the mustached man, asking him, "How 'bout you?"

The man nodded and, wincing, touched the index finger of his right hand to the tooth embedded in his lower lip and sucked a sharp breath that sounded funny through his broken nose.

Longarm picked up the mustached gent's shotgun, which had skidded down along the base of the bar. He picked it up and set it on his shoulder as he faced the room.

The men who'd been standing at the bar had all gathered toward the end of it, clumped together and staring toward Longarm. They looked hesitant, nervous, like they suddenly wanted to go home and visit with their wives.

"This is how it lays out," Longarm said, narrowing one eye with threat. "Like Melvin there probably told you, my name is Custis P. Long, Deputy United States Marshal. Your sheriff, Des Rainey, sent a telegram to my superior, Chief Marshal Billy Vail, a few weeks back, asking for help with some undisclosed situation up here in Diamondback. I was sent to investigate, so that's what I'm doin'.

"Naturally, the first person I looked for was Sheriff Rainey himself, only that's not who I found in his office. I found Melvin there, sound asleep with a cold cup of coffee in his hand. A badge way too big for him was pinned to his vest."

Little glowered at Longarm. A few of the others in

the room chuckled softly, but most of them merely sat or stood glaring at Longarm.

"I asked Melvin where I could find Sheriff Rainey and he gave me a look like a mule chewing cockleburs. Didn't learn nothin'. And that makes me right owly, not to mention suspicious as holy hell. It makes me suspicious of every one of you gents. Every person in this entire town, in fact. And I'm gonna set my boots right here in Diamondback, probably right here in the Dragoon Saloon, as well as over at that purty pink hotel yonder, until such time as I can either speak to Sheriff Rainey in person or learn exactly where he is and what he's doin' and why he requested assistance."

Longarm saw the man he'd seen earlier standing outside of the stage depot now sitting in the shadows with two other men, at a table three-quarters down the long room. He wore his green eyeshade and sleeve garters, and he stared down glumly into his nearly empty beer schooner, which he held tightly around the base with both hands.

If it were a chicken, the glass would have been dead of a broken neck by now.

"You there—what's your name?" Longarm asked the man.

The man kept staring down at his glass.

"I say, you there in the eyeshade. I take it you're the depot agent for the stage line. The telegrapher, as well—am I right?"

The man just scowled down into his beer schooner as though he were both deaf and numb. His ruddy skin behind his gray beard, however, turned crimson.

"Which means that message of Rainey's was likely

sent by you or one of your associates," Longarm persisted.

Now the gray-bearded man with the eyeshade lifted his head and swept the room with his gaze as he said, "Rainey never sent no telegraph from my key." His voice echoed around the room. He glanced at Longarm darkly and then lowered his gaze once again to his schooner.

Longarm let the man's words hang in the air. They were a lie, and he wanted to let them hang there for a time, silently incriminating everyone in the room.

Longarm's bearded attacker stirred, rolling his head from side to side and moaning into the floor. The mustached man started climbing to his feet. Longarm planted his boot on the man's ass and drove him to the floor.

"Son of a bitch!" the mustached gent said as he piled up at the base of the bar.

He glared up at Longarm. He was now holding his tooth between the thumb and index finger of his right hand as though it were something precious that he wanted to keep.

Longarm knew from all the hard stares being cast his way that no information would be forthcoming. So with a fateful sigh he turned to the bar, finished his drink in four long swallows, set the schooner back down on the bar, and ran a forearm across his mouth and mustache.

As much trail dust as beer rubbed off on his thick, brown arm. He was coated in the stuff.

A bath was due . . .

Picking up his saddlebags and his rifle, he said, "I'll

be over at the hotel yonder if anyone wants to talk to me. I'll be there till I hear anything, and since you don't have a bona fide lawman, I'll be acting as the lawman until Des Rainey returns to claim his chair. Mr. Little, that badge is no longer yours. If I see you wearing it again, I'll slap the holy living shit of you."

Melvin Little's eyes crossed slightly in rage.

"I'll be here till I find out what happened to Rainey. You fellas can rest assured of that."

The bearded man had climbed to all fours and was wagging his head and groaning loudly as he tried to rise. Longarm kicked the big man over on his back.

"As for you—you best count your lucky stars I don't haul you over to Rainey's jail and turn the key on your ugly ass. Assaulting a deputy U.S. marshal is a federal offense. That goes with you over there, too."

Longarm winked at the mustached man sitting with one knee up, his back against the bar, still holding his tooth in his hand. The front of his shirt was red with blood from his broken nose. "I see you boys armed in this town again, you'll both be getting more visits from the tooth fairy."

The bearded man spit blood at him though it merely spewed down his own chest.

Longarm swung around, pushed through the batwings, and left, knowing that he'd drawn one mighty large target on his back just now.

Chapter 8

"I'd like a room and I'd like a bath," Longarm told the big-boned, red-haired, middle-aged woman sitting behind the long, varnished oak desk in the lobby of the Diamondback Hotel.

"What—you all through makin' trouble?" the woman croaked.

She had thin lips and close-set eyes in a fleshy face that might have at one time been mildly pretty, though never beautiful. She wore a puce-colored silk dress with puffy sleeves and a scalloped cream collar. The dress fit her much too tightly, accentuating too many large bumps and rolls.

Behind her, a wooden cuckoo clock ticked on the wall above several roles of shelves and pigeonholes.

"Word sure travels fast," Longarm said, signing his name in the register book she'd turned toward him. "But there wouldn't be any trouble if the good citizens of Diamondback would just tell me what I want to know."

"Maybe the good citizens of Diamondback see the value in minding their own business."

"Is that how you see it?"

The woman only stared at him, her eyes shifting around slightly. She was a wry old bird, not all that worked up about the situation. Living out here in this rough ranch-supply settlement, she'd likely seen it all.

"That's two dollars a night. An extra fifty cents for the bath."

Longarm flipped some coins onto the open register book and said, "Where can I find the Rainey residence? I understand the sheriff is . . . or was . . . married. I'd like to talk to his wife . . . or his widow," he added meaningfully.

The woman's stony demeanor cracked abruptly and she made a sour face as she rolled her head on her broad, thick shoulders and said, "Oh, don't bring her into this! Mister, you just leave that poor woman alone. She don't know where her husband is any more than anyone else around here."

Longarm arched an eyebrow. "Why poor woman?"

"Huh?"

"You called her a 'poor' woman. Why poor? Has she become a widow recently?"

The stony mask returned to the woman's face. "Mister, you need to mind your own business just like the good folks of this town do. Mrs. Rainey don't wanna talk to you any more than anyone else does. In Diamondback, we take care of our own—private-like.

We don't need any help from the likes of you and your government badge!"

"What happened to Sheriff Rainey, Mrs . . . ?"

"Fletcher. Missus Fletcher. And your guess is as good as mine!" She swung around to pluck a key from one of the pigeonholes behind her and slapped it down on the register book. "Room fourteen."

"Does room fourteen face the street?"

"It does."

"Good. Since I'm takin' over the lawdoggin' duties in this little perdition, I'll be needing a room from where I can keep an eye on things." Longarm saw no reason to hide his frustration. He swept the key off the register book with an angry flourish, grabbed his rifle, and headed for the stairs carpeted in a rich, deep burgundy floral pattern at the lobby's rear.

His room was sparsely furnished but clean. He closed the door, set his rifle against the wall near the dresser, and set his saddlebags on the bed. He fished his bottle out of one of the pouches and poured several fingers into one of the two water glasses upended on the side of the marble-topped washstand.

He hung his dusty hat on a brass peg by the door and then walked over to the room's single window, flanking the bed. He opened the window a foot to get some fresh air into the hot, musty room and sipped the good rye as he looked down into the street.

The bearded man and the mustached man were just now being helped across the street toward a little, white-painted frame building with a large sign near its roof announcing: DOCTOR SIMON BAKER, M.D. A smaller sign near the door read: SUNDRY COMPLAINTS AND TOOTH EXTRACTIONS.

Each injured man was being guided by another—first the bearded gent and then the mustached gent. Both were limping, hatless heads hanging. A short, older, potbellied man in a vest and white shirt, likely Baker, came out of the doctor's office to stand on the stoop, watching the men angling toward him.

Longarm's keen memory reminded him that Baker had been one of the names that Melvin had mentioned when Longarm had asked the fill-in sheriff who made up the Diamondback town council. The doctor shook his head as the two injured men approached. Longarm heard him say in the otherwise quiet street, "I hope you boys got money, 'cause I don't work for free."

The bearded man was in no condition to say anything. The man guiding him led him past the sawbones and into the shack. The mustached man spat a gob of blood to one side and said, "Send the bill to Richmond."

Then he, too, was led past the doctor and into the office. The doctor followed him inside and closed the door behind him.

"Richmond," Longarm said as he lifted the glass to his lips again. That was another name that Little had mentioned.

The lawman looked around the street. Still not many folks out in the heat of the day, though shadows were beginning to bleed out from the buildings as the sun angled toward the brooding Wind River Range in the west. There were more people outside than before, however—a few clumps of men out front of the saloons, talking and drinking and casting glances toward the hotel.

Longarm threw back the last of the whiskey, set his glass on the dresser, and slid his Colt from its cross-draw holster. He flicked open the loading gate and turned the cylinder until he could see the black maw of the single empty chamber.

He always kept that chamber beneath the hammer empty so he didn't shoot himself in the leg or somewhere even more crippling. He slipped a brass-cased .44 cartridge from his shell belt, thumbed it into the chamber, flicked the loading gate closed, and spun the cylinder.

He heard voices and footsteps growing louder in the hall. Someone threw his door open without knocking. It was Mrs. Fletcher and a chubby, young Indian woman in a white apron.

Mrs. Fletcher was carrying a copper tub. She came in, announcing, "Here's your bath! Hope you're decent!"

Sitting the tub down near the door, she looked at the pistol in the lawman's hand and shook her head, her face flushed from exertion.

"You can put that away, mister. I don't care if you are calling yourself our new lawman, you won't be shootin' that hogleg in here. You do an' you can sleep out in the livery barn!"

Mrs. Fletcher turned around and walked past the portly, round-faced Indian woman, who set her steaming water buckets down and then, not looking at Longarm, her face barren of any expression whatever, dragged the tub deeper into the room. She filled it with both buckets and left, closing the door behind her.

Longarm got undressed, piled his clothes by the door, and stepped into the tub. The water was hot but not scalding, though it had promptly fogged the dresser mirror. He sat down in the water, sucking a sharp breath through his teeth as the steaming liquid seared him.

He could also feel it cut through the sweat and grit coating him. When he was good and wet, he stood, grabbed a cake of lye off the washstand, sniffed it— not overly scented, good—and lathered himself from head to toe.

In the hall, footsteps approached his door.

"Hold on a second," he said, still standing in the tub.

Too late. The Indian woman opened the door and came in with two more buckets, one steaming, one not. Longarm looked at her. She stopped in the doorway, looked at him, her almond-shaped, chocolate-dark eyes flicking up and down his brawny, soapy frame. Her eyes lingered at his crotch and then rose to his, her mouth corners quirking slightly as she set one bucket down.

She brought the other one forward and said, "Sit."

Longarm sat down in the tub.

The Indian woman poured the water over his head.

He cursed through his teeth as what felt like three layers of skin peeled off his bones.

"Mrs. Fletcher—she said to make it good an' hot," the Indian woman said. Longarm didn't look up at her, but he thought she was enjoying this. "Get the soap off. Hold on."

Longarm braced himself for the next bucket. This one was as cold as snowmelt. It must have come from one hell of a deep well.

It felt like an ice pick driven through the top of his head. It squeezed his heart like a strong, clenched fist. The ticker seemed to stop for about five seconds. When he could feel it beating again, he slid lower in the tub. The water was about right now—not too cold, not too hot.

He turned to the Indian woman, who was picking up the bucket and heading for the open door.

"Much obliged," he said through a growl.

She pointed at his clothes on the floor by the door. "Wash?"

"Please but don't let Mrs. Fletcher get her hands on 'em. She'll likely shred 'em an' that's my favorite shirt."

The Indian woman glanced over her shoulder at him, quirked another grin, and went out.

Longarm reached into the saddlebags on his bed, hauled out a little deer-hide sack containing extra smokes, and withdrew a three-for-a-nickel cheroot and a box of matches. He ran the cheroot beneath his nose, giving it a sniff, and then lit the cigar. He sagged back in the tub, drawing the smoke deep into his lungs and blowing it out at the door over his raised knees.

Smoking and lounging in the gradually cooling water, he considered the situation here in Diamondback.

It was a vexing reflection. Longarm had been sent here in response to a call for help, and the man who'd sent the missive was nowhere to be found. And no one in Diamondback would tell Longarm where he was or what had happened to him.

That meant the very worst had likely happened to

Sheriff Des Rainey. The man was probably dead, and whoever had killed him had the entire town in his iron fist. No one wanted to speak out against him. Or them.

That meant the killer had to be someone with power.

Usually, members of town councils were the most powerful men in any given town. Longarm had learned the names of the three men who sat on the Diamondback council, and he'd seen one of them a few minutes ago—Doc Baker. The others were Mulligan and Richmond. He'd look both up tomorrow. Something told him that if he sought them out today, he'd be favored with the same cold stares he'd been given since he'd first ridden into town.

All three council members likely knew Longarm was here and why. Let them stew in that for a while. Then, if Longarm was still alive in the morning—it did seem as though he was up against the whole damn town—he'd run all three men down and see what oozings he could squeeze from their hides.

Maybe nothing, but he had to try. So far, he had absolutely no clue as to why Rainey had sent that telegram to Billy Vail, or what had happened to the sheriff after he'd sent it.

That decided, Longarm reached over and grabbed his bottle off the dresser. He took a pull from the bottle, set the bottle down beside the tub, and continued to loll in the water as he smoked his cigar. The lolling must have been a soporific, because he suddenly realized that his eyes were closed.

He opened them. The room was darker, the water considerably cooler. He raised his right hand from where it had dropped down over the side of the tub.

No cigar.

He looked over the edge of the tub. The cigar had dropped onto Mrs. Fletcher's rug. It had gone out, leaving a half inch of gray ash at its tip and a small, oval-shaped charred spot in the rug.

Damn, the old biddy would likely make him pay for that—in more ways than one.

Something by the door caught his eye. Something white lay on the floor in front of it. A small scrap of paper must have been slipped beneath the door while he'd slept.

A note?

Chapter 9

Longarm frowned at the paper on the floor.

The lawman rose from the cool water, stepped out of the tub, and walked over to the small envelope that lay in front of the door. Obviously, someone had slipped it through the crack beneath the door while he'd slept.

He picked it up and shook out the piece of paper tucked inside. It was a small slip of cream-colored parchment—the kind that ladies used to send thank-you notes. He opened it.

There were two sentences inked beautifully in flowing, feminine cursive: "Come to room nineteen after midnight and your questions will be answered. Do not tell a soul."

Longarm sniffed the paper. It smelled like lavender and lilac.

He tapped the note on the envelope as he thought about it, and then slipped the note back into the envelope, set it on the dresser, and pulled a clean change of clothes out of his saddlebags.

A trap? Nah, not in Mrs. Fletcher's hotel. Not entirely out of the question, but he was more likely to get bushwhacked outside after dark.

His change of clothes consisted of an outfit identical to the one the chubby Indian girl had hauled away—frock coat, blue chambray shirt, string tie, fawn-gold vest, and skintight tweed trousers. The duds were a little wrinkled from riding folded up in his saddlebags, but the wrinkles would plane out the longer he walked around.

And walk was just what he intended to do tonight. Not only to kill time before knocking on the door of the mysterious room 19, but to get the general lay of the land. A man never knew what he could learn just by walking around a town.

He'd have supper, a few drinks, and then he'd walk around some more.

Besides, he'd deemed himself the local law in Des Rainey's stead, so it was more or less his job to keep an eye on things, maybe turn the jailhouse key on a few drunks. True, he was likely to attract trouble, but he wasn't going to learn anything about Rainey by hiding under his bed. And anyway, he had a pretty good sense about trouble.

He'd be keeping that cylinder under his gun hammer filled with brass even at the risk of shooting his pecker off. And he'd haul his Winchester around even at risk of looking like an asshole.

He brushed the trail dust from his hat and set it on

his head, tipping it down over his right eye, cavalry style. He stuffed three cheroots into his shirt pocket, grabbed his rifle, and headed out.

Since over the last few hours his belly had been getting far too friendly with his backbone, he walked east along the street until he saw the two-story wood-frame building he'd seen on his way into town earlier. Half the place belonged to a saddle, harness, and gun shop while the other half wore a shingle over its front door announcing ABIGAILE'S CAFÉ.

The sun was not yet down, but smoke puffed from the tin chimney pipe poking up out of the café's roof, rife with the smell of roasting meat and burning pine. Three horses stood at the hitchrack fronting the place, and that was more than were now parked in front of any of the saloons.

That told Longarm that Abigaile's was likely a favorite local feed sack. The Diamondback Hotel had a restaurant, but Longarm wanted to check out another place by way of getting his boots wet in the mysterious little town obviously brimming with nasty secrets.

He went inside, and the three cowboys sitting at a table in the room's center looked at him and grew as quiet as church mice.

Longarm sat down at a table a little farther back of the three waddies, where he could keep an eye on them as well as the door. A penciled card on the table covered in red-and-white checked oilcloth gave him two choices—pork roast or roasted chicken. After the sullen-looking blond girl of about sixteen came out of the kitchen to take his order, looking him over skeptically—she'd obviously heard who and what he was, along with everyone else in town by now—she headed back toward the kitchen.

The cowboys hadn't said a word since Longarm walked into the café, but they all watched the girl's nice round ass behind her simple gray skirt as she sashayed past their table and pushed through the swing door to the kitchen. One snickered and another one pulled the hat down over the third one's eyes.

They said nothing before they finished their meal, belched, and left. Once outside, they discussed which saloon they were going to patronize that evening, and then swung up into their saddles and gave several revelrous whoops as they galloped west.

Longarm enjoyed the pork roast with all the trimmings—mashed potatoes bathed in rich, dark gravy, green beans, a sliced tomato, a fresh-from-the-oven bun, which he broke open and liberally applied butter to, and a small dessert of peaches sliced in sugar. He washed it all down with a glass of milk and piping hot black coffee, and then sat back in his chair, belched, and loosened his belts a notch.

When the girl came back out of the kitchen to stride lazily to Longarm's table, canting her head to one side, she said, "That'll be two bits, mister. The advice is free."

Longarm reached into his pants pocket as he looked up at her. "Oh? What advice might that be?"

She set her hands on the table and leaned forward. She didn't seem to mind that her dress hung out away from her chest to give a man who was predisposed to peek a look at her creamy breasts jostling down inside her cotton chemise. "You best break a leg gettin' outta here," she said in a syrupy thick Southern accent.

"Why would that be, sweetheart? Everyone here seems so nice."

"You'll find out how nice they are."

"Anything else you wanna tell me?"

The girl glanced over her shoulder toward the kitchen, where someone—Abigaile?—was banging pots and pans around.

"I'd tell you where you could find me later, after Aunt Abigaile goes to bed, but you might not be around long enough to take what I'd offer." She straightened, letting her eyes flick across his shoulders and then down toward his crotch. "Shame, too. You're a long, tall drink of water, mister. I bet you could really stoke a lonely girl's firebox."

With that, she shoved the money Longarm had given her down her dress, picked up his plate, glass, and cup, and, giving him a coolly coquettish parting glance, swung around to sashay back into the kitchen, her round hips looking like two dogs straining at their chains.

Longarm stared at the girl's ass. She wanted him to, after all, and he only felt it right to oblige her. Her youth and beauty reminded him of Connie. His interlude with the auburn-haired, green-eyed beauty seemed a long time ago now, but he still couldn't help wondering, in a vague sort of way, if it had really happened or if he'd merely been dreaming.

At the moment he had too much on his plate to worry about it. Bigger fish to fry.

Returning his focus to Sheriff Rainey, he scooped his rifle off the chair beside him and rose from the table. He reached into his shirt pocket for a cheroot and stuck it between his teeth. As he stepped outside, he paused on the narrow stoop to reach into his coat pocket for a match.

The sun had gone down and this broad basin was filled with velvety darkness. The Wind Rivers were jutting black silhouettes in the west, shouldering back against the fast-fading lilac that was all that remained of the day.

All was quiet. Diamondback had settled in for the evening.

Soon, though, Longarm knew, the hands from near ranches would be making their way to the town's saloons. Some already had, for several horses stood tied to each of the town's watering holes, lamps from the respective saloons flashing dully off bridle bits and saddle trimmings.

Longarm fired the match on his thumbnail and cupped it to the cigar. The flame expanded and contracted as smoke wafted around his head. When the cheroot was drawing to his satisfaction, he tossed the match into the dirt beyond the stoop and continued to pull the smoke into his lungs, watching the coal glow at the end of the cigar.

The glowing coal disappeared all too suddenly. Longarm felt the cigar jerk between his lips. At the same time, he saw a wicked flash of orange-blue light to his right, and a quarter second later the blast of the rifle reached his ears, echoing shrilly.

Longarm let the cigar slip from between his lips and he swung, raising his rifle in both hands as he levered a fresh cartridge into the chamber.

Boom!—Boom!—Boom!

His own rifle blasts sounded like ignited barrels of dynamite under the stoop's low roof. Inside the café, someone screamed and dropped a pan with a raucous clatter.

Longarm watched a shadow jostle east, away from where he'd seen the rifle flash. In the corner of his left eye he caught the movement of another shadow against a gray storefront. He threw himself over the porch rail on his left as a sharp pop sounded across the street, and more gun flames lapped toward him.

The slug hammered into a porch rail.

Longarm rolled off a shoulder and rose to his left hip, slamming the Winchester's stock against his side and cutting loose. The rifle leaped and roared four times. After the second shot, he'd heard a man's shrill curse and watched the second dry-gulcher's pistol fire into the street.

Longarm lowered the Winchester and saw the man-shaped shadow slumped in the street fronting the gray storefront. The shadow wasn't moving. Longarm was pretty sure he'd hit the bastard with all four rounds. He'd danced this jig before, so his instincts were keen.

He tossed the rifle down and ran around the front of the porch, crouching as he headed east. He saw the jostling shadow of the man who'd blown the coal off his cigar, heard the man's boots thudding on a board-walk about fifty yards east of Abigaile's.

Longarm ground his low-heeled boots into the dirt, propelling himself forward in a full sprint.

He lost sight of the man, but then a flash and a shrill crack placed the bushwhacker. The slug curled the air about six inches left of Longarm's head. The lawman stopped running and triggered his .44 three times, hoping like hell no one was in the dark shop flanking the man he was shooting at.

He held fire, ran forward, and dropped to a knee, peering out from beneath a hitchrack toward the spot from which he'd been fired upon. He heard a raspy, strained breath, saw the bushwhacker's shadow rise, fall back against a white-painted frame building, and then twist and dash around the building's far corner.

Longarm had wounded the man.

He crouched through the hitchrack and ran along beside two more building fronts before he gained the low, white-frame building—a land office. He stole quietly up to the far end, doffed his hat, and peered around the corner.

A rifle thundered, stabbing orange flames.

Longarm jerked his head back as the slug thumped loudly into the side of the building just right of where his face had been a moment before.

The image of the shooter revealed by his gun's flash was still dancing across his retinas. Hearing the man running, Longarm quickly jerked his pistol around the corner again and saw the shooter's shadow shuffling, sort of crouching and dragging one foot, toward the rear of the next building.

"Stop or take it in the back, you son of a bitch! Your call!"

The man stopped, wheeled. Ambient light flashed off the rifle he was raising.

Longarm emptied his .44, and then, flicking the loading gate open and shaking out the six spent car-

tridge casings, he casually walked around the corner
of the land office and into the break between that
building and the next one. It was a fifteen-foot gap littered with old lumber, a rusty wagon wheel, newspa-
pers, and airtight tins. His quarry lay on his back,
brown hat beside him, both arms stretched out. The
barrel of the rifle had squashed his hat crown.

The shooter was still breathing, flat belly rising and
falling sharply. He was wheezing. Longarm recognized a death rattle when he heard one. Blood shone
dark on his cream shirt and tan vest. The bullets that
had torn into his back had ripped right through him.

Longarm recognized the attire and the blond, fair-
skinned features of one of the three drovers he'd seen
in Abigaile's. That meant that the other dead bushwhacker was from the same trio.

Why?

Longarm looked toward each end of the alley, wary
of the third man. Neither spying nor hearing anyone
else, he dropped to a knee beside the dying man and
asked, "Who put you up to this?"

The kid—Longarm figured he wasn't much past
twenty—was wincing and gritting his teeth against
the pain of his imminent death.

"You . . . you kilt me, you son of a bitch . . . !" was
all he said.

His belly stopped moving. He let out one last, long
sigh, his life riding away on the plume of expelled air.
Then he lay still. The whites in his eyes glistened in
the light of the kindling stars.

Behind Longarm, in the direction of the street,
voices rose. So did the sound of several sets of

fast-moving footsteps. A light washed across the street. Men—quite a few men—were moving toward the lawman.

Longarm straightened, finished punching fresh shells into his Colt's cylinder, then slid the loading gate closed and spun the wheel. Holding the pistol straight out in front of him, he started walking toward the street, ready to meet the next storm gun barrel first.

Chapter 10

"Hold your fire! Hold your goddamn fire!"

The angry voice had come from the street. It belonged to one of the group headed up by a man in a gunmetal-gray business suit carrying a railroad lantern by its wire handle.

The lantern cast a glow over the front of the group, which appeared to be comprised of between a half a dozen and ten men all sticking close to the heels of the bowler-hatted leader holding the lantern up even with his head.

"I will if you will," Longarm said, holding his pistol straight out from his right side, aimed warningly at the group.

The man with the lantern stopped. He wore small round spectacles and a pewter mustache. Hair of the same color shone beneath his crisp, black bowler and in the sideburns dropping down the sides of his face.

He was an elegant, dapper dude in a twenty-dollar suit no doubt tailor-made for his compact frame.

The others stopped close behind him. They reminded Longarm of a gaggle of ducklings following close on their mother's tail feathers.

"What in the name of God is going on?" barked the dapper gent, lifting his gaze from Longarm's pistol.

"You tell me."

The man glared at Longarm from behind his glasses that reflected the lantern light and thus hid his eyes. "Ah," he said. "You're the man I've been hearing so much about. Deputy Long, I take it?"

"Who're you?"

"Alexander Richmond, owner and president of the Diamondback Valley Bank and Trust. Also mayor and head of the town council."

"Just the man I've been wanting to talk to," Longarm said. "Figured maybe you could tell me why those two were fixin' to drill me with a third eye and a third ear hole, neither of which I'd be able to see or hear through."

"They shot at you?"

"Indeed they did."

"Who are they?"

"You tell me, Mr. Mayor."

One of the men from the rear of the group piped up with "Giff Berkley's the dead one outside the feed store, Mr. Richmond."

"And there's another down there?" Richmond asked Longarm, lifting his chin to indicate the alley behind the lawman.

"Yep."

Richmond turned his regal head to one side. "Two of you men check it out."

Two men separated from the group and jogged into the break behind Longarm. Longarm kept his head forward, making sure none of the nine men before him decided to try and finish the job the other two had started.

Shortly, one of the men behind him yelled, "Cletus Delphi!"

"Delphi and Berkley," Richmond said, working the names around between his lips. "Aren't they on Tanner Webster's roll?"

"Sure are," said one of the men behind Richmond. The group had fanned out a little. None were holding guns, but most were armed, and they regarded Longarm with expressions running the gamut between jeering and bald hatred.

"Who's Tanner Webster?" Longarm wanted to know.

"A big rancher in these parts, Deputy Long. He owns half the basin. He's not going to be at all happy to see two of his horses return to his ranch with empty saddles."

"Maybe I should ride out and apologize."

Since no one else appeared to be holding a weapon, Longarm lowered his six-shooter and walked up to within two feet of Richmond. The banker/mayor was in his mid-to-late fifties—an even-featured, shrewd, intelligent man who considered himself head and shoulders above all others. One who'd likely been born with an arrogant cast to his gaze and would die with same.

"Don't get smart with me, Deputy Long. I'm not

afraid of you. Just because you wear the badge of deputy U.S. marshal doesn't mean—"

"It means I'm gonna get the answer to a few questions," Longarm said through his teeth. "The first one is, where is Sheriff Rainey? The second one is, why every time I ask about him do the good citizens of Diamondback swallow their tongues? My guess is Rainey's dead. That leaves a third question. Who killed him?"

Richmond ground his jaws together. "You're just full of questions, aren't you?"

Longarm could only laugh.

That seemed to antagonize Richmond even more. With his free hand he jutted a bony finger at the federal lawman. "All that you need to know, mister, is this town takes care of its own problems. We don't need the interference of the federal government. This is a local matter, and we—all of the good citizens of Diamondback—will be very pleased to see you ride out of our town tomorrow morning at first light."

"No."

"What?" Richmond said through one half of his mouth, turning his head slightly askance.

"I'm the law in this town now, Richmond. Whether you like it or not. And I'll be here until I find out what happened to Rainey. If he's dead, I intend to bring his killer or killers to justice—and that goes for anyone else involved—such as the one who called the shots. I'll only be leavin' here when I've finished that task. Only then."

"You think so, do you?" Richmond barked, glasses

glinted furiously in the lantern light. "Well, you might just have another think comin', mister!"

Richmond wheeled and ordered several men to find any more of Tanner Webster's men in town, and to have them haul their dead back to the Flying W for burial. Then Richmond cast Longarm another glare over his shoulder and strode off down the street to the west.

"I'll be talkin' to you later, Richmond," Longarm called after him. "And I'll be getting some answers if I have to beat them out of you."

Richmond stopped abruptly, turned sideways, and looked back at Longarm in shock. Unaccustomed to being addressed in such a fashion, he apparently could think of no suitable retort to the threat. He merely smacked his jaws together and strode off down the street, the others flanking him and fanning out to whatever saloon they'd been drinking in when they'd seen the banker headed east with his lantern.

Longarm walked back to Abigaile's and picked up his rifle. Two men from Richmond's group were hauling the dead man from in front of the feed store east along the north side of the street, grunting under the weight of their burden. Longarm picked up his rifle, wiped dust and horseshit from the barrel, breech, and both stocks, and reloaded the weapon.

His heart was still racing—from the anxiety of the lead swap, which not even the most seasoned lawmen enjoyed getting into on a dark night, but also from rage and frustration. He didn't know when the last time was that he'd felt this confounded.

A whole town full of people who likely knew what

had happened to their sheriff, but not one of them was willing to tell. None seemed to bat an eye's worth of respect for Longarm's position as deputy United States marshal. It made him feel impotent, useless, and discombobulated beyond imagining.

If there was a dog nearby, he'd probably kick it. And he'd never kicked a dog before in his life, had never even imagined feeling inclined to do so.

He set the loaded rifle on his shoulder, fished his old railroad turnip out of his vest pocket, and flipped the lid. Only nine-thirty. He still had nearly three hours before his appointment with whoever had slipped that note under his door.

He decided to take a swing around the town, to get the lay of the land. He was the new lawman of Diamondback, after all, and he should know how the buildings were laid out.

After he'd walked once around the town, which only took a half hour since it wasn't very large, he stopped by the Dragoon Saloon for a beer and a shot of tarantula juice. His presence seemed to stymie the watering hole's festive night atmosphere, and all the other people there, including the dark, pock-faced bartender, looked like they hadn't taken a decent shit in a month of Sundays.

It was the same with the other two saloons in town—the High Country Inn and the Ace-High. As soon as the dark, rangy lawman in the three-piece suit walked in, the hum of conversation dropped several notches, and it didn't pick up again until Longarm had passed through the batwings once more and walked out into the fresh air of the night-cloaked main street.

The town had quieted considerably after eleven o'clock, it being a weeknight. But Longarm took another turn around Diamondback, mostly in stubborn defiance of another ambush. Though he was spoiling for a fight, none came, and he couldn't say he was sorry it hadn't.

Frustration a hot fire burning at the base of his spine, the lawman returned to the hotel. He'd been so preoccupied with the town that he'd almost forgotten about his invitation to room 19.

He walked through the hotel lobby and past the front desk. Mrs. Fletcher wasn't there—the old biddy had probably gone to bed at nine. Longarm was glad she'd left the door unlocked. In his sour, frustrated mood, he'd likely have shot the glass out of the door's upper pane. That might have been overstepping his bounds slightly.

His rifle resting on his shoulder, he headed up the carpeted steps. He passed his own floor and headed up the last flight to the third floor. As he walked down the hall lit by a couple of smoky bracket-lamps, he freed the keeper thong from over the hammer of his .44.

The rifle was best for out in the open. The pistol was more effective at close quarters, and if he'd been led into another ambush, a hotel room would be close quarters indeed.

He stopped at room 19, which was at the far end of the third-floor hall, and lightly tapped his knuckles on the door. The latch clicked immediately. The door drew back until there was a one-inch gap between the door and the frame.

A pair of hazel eyes peered out at him. A feminine voice whispered, "Marshal Long?"

"That's right."

Stepping back, she drew the door open. Longarm's knees nearly buckled at the delectable creature standing before him—a young, high-busted, classically featured young woman with honey-blond hair piled loosely atop her head. She wore what appeared a series of thin, lace-edged housecoats over a more rustic man's underwear top that was buttoned up to her fine, slender neck.

"Please come in," she said, her voice trembling slightly.

Her wide hazel eyes owned an emotional sheen. She was pale, and she looked exhausted. In fact, she looked a little haggard, which somehow accentuated her natural, earthy beauty. She wore no face paint whatever, and her heart-shaped features, with short nose and wide-set, innocent eyes, made her look even younger than he thought she was—mid-to-late twenties. And more fragile.

Longarm quickly glanced around the room behind her. Seeing no one else there, and nothing out of sorts, he stepped forward. She closed the door behind him and leaned into it as though she were too tired to stand without assistance.

Longarm turned to her, frowning, puzzled. "And you're . . . ?"

Still leaning against the door, the young woman turned to him, the light of a single lit lamp on a side table reflected in her eyes, which seemed to own a perpetual sheen of tears. "Mrs. Rainey. Mrs. Desmond Rainey."

"Oh."

She quirked her mouth corners, though no humor touched her sad eyes. "I know—I'm considerably younger than Des was."

"Was."

"Oh, he's dead. I thought maybe you'd figured that out by now. I'd heard from Mrs. Fletcher that you were a marshal."

"Deputy marshal."

"Whatever." She turned from the door and leaned against it, sliding her shoulders back slightly. He couldn't help glancing at the full bosom jutting toward him, though a pang of guilt shot through him for noting it. The poor woman was obviously a wreck, and here he was admiring her tits.

If that wasn't just like him.

"I'm sorry . . . Mrs. Rainey."

He knew he must have looked like he'd swallowed a horseshoe. Nothing could have surprised him more than finding out that the sheriff of Diamondback, who'd been nearly as old as Chief Marshal Billy Vail, was married to such a striking, young beauty.

Mentally he tried to shake off his confusion and get down to brass tacks.

"How?" he asked.

Chapter 11

Mrs. Rainey turned her head toward the door as though listening. "I think Mrs. Fletcher has gone to bed. The only other boarder is a traveling salesman, and I'm sure he doesn't care about any of this."

She turned to Longarm again and drew a heavy breath. "You won't be needing the rifle, Marshal. Can I offer you a drink?"

"Why not?"

She moved to the side table on which the single lantern burned. Longarm leaned his rifle against the wall by the door, looked around, and saw that he was in the sitting room of what appeared to be a two-room suite.

This parlor area, papered in purple above dark-stained pine wainscoting, was about twice the size of Longarm's room. It was simply, comfortably furnished with a couch, a brocade-upholstered armchair, and a rocking chair arranged around a stylish area rug.

A charcoal brazier glowed in a corner. The door to the bedroom was open, revealing an unmade bed with a candle burning on a near table. The bed was rumpled, covers thrown back. Longarm had a feeling that Rainey's bereaved widow had been spending a lot of time in it.

Her hands shook slightly as she splashed amber liquid from a cut glass container into two short water glasses. She brought one of the glasses to Longarm.

"Brandy," she said. "Probably not the appropriate glass, but my husband never stood much on form, which was one of the things I loved about him."

Her voice quavered and tears oozed into her eyes. She smiled as though to try to cover the emotion, and swung around quickly. She walked over and retrieved the other glass and then walked over to the rocking chair. Turning to Longarm, she held out her arm and said, "Please. Have a seat."

She sat down in the rocker. She appeared to be struggling to maintain composure.

She knew what he wanted to know, so Longarm sat down in the armchair, sipped his brandy, and waited. She sipped her own drink and crossed one leg over the other.

"He was shot," she said, staring at the floor between them, rocking a little in the chair.

She drew a breath, steeling herself. "I saw it happen. I was here, waiting for him as I always do, every afternoon. We always went to supper together downstairs or we'd walk over to Abigaile's. Five-thirty every evening. I knew he'd ridden out of town earlier, and I'd been worried all day. I had a . . . I don't know . . .

a funny feeling in the pit of my stomach. I remember I even prayed and I, like Des, was never given to prayer. I was raised in a very strict, religious household, and I'd had enough . . ."

Mrs. Rainey shook her head, apparently realizing she was getting off track.

She took another sip of her brandy and lifted her gaze to Longarm. "Like I said, Marshal Long—I saw it happen. I was at the window. It was raining and Des was walking up to the jailhouse. He must have just gotten back to town and stabled his horse. He went into the sheriff's office and a moment later there a flash in the windows and in the door. I thought maybe Des was having trouble with a lamp, but then I saw him . . ."

The woman's voice quivered. She lowered her gaze to the floor again and lifted a shaky hand to her face.

She pressed two fingers to her chin, drew a breath, and then pinched her chin between her thumb and index finger. "I saw Des fly back out of the office and land in the street." Her breasts rose and fell heavily as her breathing became strained. "He landed in the muddy street."

"Someone was waiting in the office for him?"

She nodded. Her face crumpled, but then she got her emotions under control again. She swallowed. "Yes. I heard the blast. It sounded like thunder. Funny, I thought for a minute lightning had struck his office. I stared at him just lying there, not quite able to believe what I was seeing, and then I ran out of the room and down the stairs. I screamed for Mrs. Fletcher and ran outside."

Her mouth twisted. Tears streamed down her cheeks.

"By the time I got to him, he was dead. He just stared up at me. It almost looked like he was smiling, as though he were telling me not to worry, that everything would be all right."

Mrs. Rainey's voice broke, and the rest came out pinched and barely understandable: "But he was dead though his eyes were still open. He was dead! Des was dead and just lying there in the street!"

She leaned forward, elbows resting on her knees, and cried into her hands.

She looked so grieved and vulnerable and down-right tortured that Longarm, awkward at lending comfort, rose from his chair and dropped to a knee before her. She was sobbing uncontrollably. He touched her arm, and it seemed to be the only invitation she needed to lean into him, wrap her arms around him, and bury her wet face in his shoulder.

Now she cried harder, her body spasming against him.

Longarm wrapped his arms around her and held her until her cries slowly died. She pulled her head away, and Longarm dug a handkerchief out of his pants pocket.

"Thanks," she whispered, wiping her cheeks and brushing the cloth across her nose. "I'm so sorry."

"No, ma'am," Longarm said gently. "I'm the one who's sorry. But if it's any consolation at all, I aim to find out who killed your husband and bring him to justice. Do you have any idea?"

"Yes." She nodded, blowing her nose into his handkerchief.

The firm reply startled him.

She sat back in her chair, balling his handkerchief

in her fist. "I'll have this cleaned for you, Deputy Long."

"Please, call me Longarm." He realized that he had his hand on her knee. He removed it quickly, though he could still feel the warmth of her supple leg. She looked at his hand, as well, in a vague, oblique way, and then lifted her glass to her lips and sipped the brandy.

As she set the glass back down, she looked at him still on one knee before her and frowned. "Longarm?"

Longarm offered a sheepish smile. "Custis Long, long arm of the law. I reckon that's where it comes from. I been called Longarm so long I reckon I plumb forgot exactly where the handle came from. All I know is that's what most folks call me, and you're welcome to call me that, too."

She smiled as brightly as she could through her anguish. "Longarm. I like that. Please call me Meg."

"All right, Meg." Without realizing that he had raised his hand again, he placed it on her knee. It seemed the natural thing to do, so he tried not to pay too much attention to it as he said, "You said you know who the killer might be. Did you see him?"

Meg Rainey shook her head. "No. By the time I'd run out there, he was gone. I saw someone run around the corner of the building just west of my husband's office, but it was cloudy and rainy and he was just a blur. I believe he was wearing a black hat and a cream shirt, possibly a red neckerchief, but I could be wrong about all of that." She shook her head once, blinking. "I'd hate to accuse the wrong man. I really want you to find the man who killed my husband, Deputy Long. The right man."

"And who might that be?"

"I don't know for sure. But I suspect—Oh, I shouldn't say this without more proof . . ." She set her left elbow on an arm of the rocker and rested her chin against the heel of the hand in which Longarm's handkerchief was wadded.

Longarm gently squeezed her knee. "Please, Meg— any information you can give me will be a whole wagonload more than what I have so far . . ."

"All I can really tell you for now, Longarm, is that someone rode to town that morning to fetch my husband on what sounded like a dire mission. I was in Des's office—we often took our coffee together around eight—and Dan Garvey's hired hand, a drunkard named Calvin Johnson, galloped into town to inform Des that his boss wanted to see him out at the crossroads near Diamondback Creek. Apparently he'd discovered something that Des needed to look into."

"A killing? Rustling?"

"I have no idea." She stopped, reconsidered. "I mean, I do have an idea, but I'd like you to look into the matter first before I offer it. Because I could be wrong, and the last thing I want to do is accuse the wrong people of murdering Des." She stared at him, and he felt the burn of her hazel gaze. "The right man—or men—must be brought to justice."

Longarm sighed and rose, throwing back the last of his brandy and thinking through what Meg had told him. She held her empty glass up. "Would you mind?" she asked.

"Not at all."

"Refill your own, as well."

Longarm went over to the side table and splashed another two shots into each glass. He brought Meg's back to her, sipped his own, and looked down at the poor woman, who continued to seem on the verge of breaking down.

"I guess, since you won't give me the name of the man you suspect, I'll have to ride out to this Garvey place and see what the trouble had been the day your husband was killed."

Meg nodded. Tears came to her eyes, and she winced and looked away. "I'll draw you a map," she said, her voice quivering. She set her elbow on the arm of her chair again and leaned her forehead against her fist. "Oh, Des," she said, "why did this have to happen?"

Longarm knelt before her again, placed his hand on her knee. This time it was purely an automatic gesture stemming from his desire to lend comfort. "I'm very sorry, Mrs.—Meg. Isn't there someone in town who can stay with you until you're feeling better?"

"Mrs. Fletcher offered, but it didn't feel right. People in town—they . . . well, they don't seem to want to have much to do with me. It's almost like they all feel guilty about Des's murder. It's as though they somehow feel responsible for it—because I suppose they suspect who did it—and I only remind them of the trouble."

She stared at him, befuddled. "Do you know what I mean, Longarm?"

"I know what you mean. No one in town—aside

from you, of course—has offered me any help at all
in finding Sheriff Rainey's killer. I was beginning to
suspect the entire town was somehow responsible. That
they'd all turned on the man they'd hired to enforce
the laws here in Diamondback."

"No, that's not it. They're just afraid of what might
happen to the town when the real killer or killers are
brought to justice."

"So it is someone powerful, then."

"I think so. But that's all I want to say on the matter. If I talk too much, I could influence your investigation in the wrong way. And I don't want to do that.
I want you to investigate this yourself, knowing only
what I told you."

"You think that's enough, Meg?"

"I do." She placed her hand on his hand that was
resting on her knee. "I will be very anxious to learn
what you come up with, Longarm."

Longarm looked at their hands. He was conscious
of the warm and supple leg beneath his palm. He slid
his hand out from beneath hers and started to rise.
"Well, I'd best get on back to my own—"

"Please, stay."

Chapter 12

Longarm remained on his knee, frowning up at the woman. He wasn't sure he'd heard her correctly.

"You'll think me craven, but I don't want to be alone tonight."

"But, Meg . . ."

"I'm so tired of feeling only pain, Longarm. I'd like to feel something else besides pain, pain, pain! Do you understand?"

"I think you're just—"

"It's no secret that my husband was much older than I. We were married only two years. For one year, he . . ." She glanced off as though searching for the right words. "He wasn't the man he wanted to be. Make no mistake, I loved Des dearly, and I managed to suppress my natural needs. I didn't want him to feel any worse than he already felt. But . . ."

She raked her arms across Longarm's thick,

weathered-brown neck and his broad chest and heavy shoulders straining the seams of his frock coat. "But . . . you're here now, and I must tell you, as shameful as it may be, I thoroughly enjoyed your hand on my knee just now."

Longarm's heart thudded.

He opened his mouth to speak, but she leaned forward suddenly and placed two fingers to his lips.

"Please, put it on my knee again, will you?" she whispered.

Longarm finished his drink in one fell swoop, set the glass on the floor, and placed his hand on her knee again. It was warmer than before. He felt as though he could feel it expanding and contracting with each beat of her heart. He could hear her breathing as she stared down at his hand, tears slowly rolling down her cheeks from wet eyes.

She placed her hand on his hand again, very gently. Slowly, she pressed it more firmly on his. She breathed harder and harder, her breasts rising and falling heavily behind her thin, colorful wraps and the man's cream undershirt.

"Take your cock out of your pants," she breathed, keeping her eyes on her hand pressing firmly down on his.

"Meg, maybe we should think about this. I'm not sure you're thinking clearly." As much as he wanted this woman—as much as she'd worked him up, he had no intention of taking advantage of her in this obviously precarious, emotionally compromised state she was in.

"Take your cock out of your pants. I want to see it."

Longarm swallowed. Her words alone were flooding blood to the organ of topic.

He straightened, unbuckled his cartridge belt, and set it on the chair he'd been sitting on. She was leaning forward a little in her rocking chair, hands folded together in her lap, staring at his crotch.

Her eyes were like warm fingers stroking him. His pants and summer-weight balbriggans were growing painfully tight.

Longarm unbuttoned the top button of his pants. She parted her lips.

He unbuttoned his three fly buttons, and a lock of hair slid down from the knot she'd gathered it in, to dangle along her cheek. Longarm felt foolish about exposing himself to this woman he'd just met, but he was also almost erect and getting more erect nearly as fast as a snake could strike. There was something so erotically charged about this grief-stricken woman that there was no turning back.

He peeled his pants open and then lowered his summer underwear. His cock bounced free of its confines and hung at half-mast though it was swelling noticeably, nearly as thick and round as a bung starter.

"Oh, my god," Meg whispered.

Leaning forward, she slowly reached out, turning her hand palm upward, thumb extended, and caressed the underside of the nodding, growing organ. She placed her other hand on his balls, kneading them with her fingers. She turned the first hand and wrapped her fingers around his cock that was, by now, standing up and arcing back against his belly.

She smiled and pumped him slowly, gently, fingering

his balls with her other hand, leaning forward very slowly until her lips were touching the head of his cock. She kept them there for a time while she played with him, and then she opened her lips slightly and kissed him.

Her tongue slithered out of her mouth, and she licked the swollen, purple head.

Longarm groaned, gritted his teeth. Her tongue was like a pure blue flame. Desire stabbed up from his balls and deep into his belly, making his heart beat heavier, faster.

Meg slid forward from her chair and dropped to her knees. She released his cock and, staring up at him with tender eyes pleading for understanding as well as for nourishment of her long pent-up desires, she slid her wraps down her shoulders.

She unbuttoned the cream undershirt and let it, too, fall from her shoulders, revealing her full breasts, creamy and tender, round as medium-sized cantaloupes, pink nipples jutting.

Longarm's spine melted. His cock throbbed harder, standing straight out in front of his flat, corded belly, nodding.

She smiled up at him beguilingly, and then wrapped her right hand around his massive cock once more. She cupped her other hand beneath his heavy balls and then closed her mouth over the head of his cock. She moved her face first to one side, then the other, sliding him against the inside of each cheek, causing each cheek to bulge.

She licked and sucked and then went so far down on him that he thought he could feel her heart throbbing against his staff's swollen head. She gagged deep in her chest and then slid her mouth off of him, gasping, spittle stringing between her lips and his member.

"It's so big," she said throatily, staring wide-eyed at the wet member standing at attention in front of her face.

She swallowed, licked some spittle from his cock, and lifted her eyes to his. "I'd like it deeper inside me, Longarm. Could you do that for me and not think me a monster? I have a feeling that Des would understand." She narrowed her eyes slightly and quirked her mouth corners. "In fact, I bet he's smiling down from Heaven right now, giving us both permission."

She'd obviously loved her husband a great deal, but Longarm thought that grief had chewed a large hole in her brain. But if there was no stopping himself before, there certainly was no stopping him now.

"Stand up," he croaked. "Let me get a good look at you, Meg."

She kept ahold of his cock as she rose and stood before him, sliding her shoulders back, breasts out. She gave a shudder of desire. Chicken flesh covered both bosoms, and the nipples tightened, distended even farther.

Longarm kissed her rich mouth and placed his hands on her breasts, cupping them, kneading them, rolling the nipples beneath his thumbs. He wrapped his arms around her and kissed her more passionately. She groaned and released his cock and wrapped her arms around his neck, mashing her wet lips against his, flicking her tongue into his mouth and pressing it against his own.

Finally, he released her, stepped back, and shrugged out of his coat.

Her breasts rose and fell as she met his fervent, passionate gaze with one of her own. She slipped out of the pantaloons that were all that she was wearing now, and while he undressed, she picked up their empty brandy glasses and walked over to the side table.

He watched her, letting his eyes feast on her pale, long-limbed, full-hipped body, the half-moons of her breasts bulging out from beneath her arms. She filled their glasses, glanced at him, smiled, and then walked across the parlor area and through the door to the bedroom.

Longarm grabbed his shell belt and holster and followed her. Inside the bedroom, she sat on the bed, holding her drink against her cleavage. Her eyes no longer owned the emotional sheen of before. Now they danced and shone smoky with a cool, feminine passion, the nubs of her cheeks lightly brushed with pink.

"Any second thoughts?" he asked, as he coiled his cartridge belt around his holster and set the gun rig on the dresser where the single candle burned.

"None. I want you to fuck me hard. I want you to make me forget, at least for tonight, the anguish that burns inside me. Will you do that, Longarm? And then will you find the man who murdered my husband?"

She reached out and stroked his cock, looking up at him from beneath her auburn brows.

Longarm placed his hands on her shoulders. "For the rest of the night, Meg, you won't have to think about one other thing except my cock inside you."

He gently shoved her back on the bed, wrapped his

arms around her, and slid her up against her pillow. Slowly, tenderly, he mounted her. And then he went to work with abandon.

Several times he had to clamp his hand over Meg's mouth to keep her screams from waking Mrs. Fletcher and the drummer. When he'd taken her once, he turned her over, slid the pillow beneath her hips, and pounded her hard from behind.

They frolicked for nearly three hours, sipping brandy. Then they both slept. At the first birdcry of the false dawn, Longarm rose quietly in the still-dark room and dressed. As he strapped his gunbelt around his waist and headed for the door, Meg stirred.

"Longarm?" she said drowsily, still half asleep.

"Yeah?"

"Thank you."

Longarm went back and kissed her warm, soft cheek. "My honor as well as my pleasure."

"You'll find him?" she asked, opening her eyes and gazing up at him gravely. "Des's killer."

"Count on it."

He kissed her cheek once more and then strode out of the bedroom and into the sitting room. He retrieved his rifle from where he'd leaned it against the wall by the door, and left.

He'd no sooner drawn the door closed behind him than something cold, round, and hard was pressed against his right ear. There was the crisp, decisive sound of a gun hammer being ratcheted back.

"I'm about to save this town a whole lot of misery," a raspy voice said in the same ear that the pistol was pressed against.

Chapter 13

The breath wafting against Longarm's right cheek was rife with the smell of chaw and whiskey. It was accompanied by the old man smell of sour sweat and hair oil. In the corner of Longarm's right eye, he glimpsed the edge of a green eyeshade and a gray beard.

"Come on," the old man said, pressing the pistol barrel harder against Longarm's ear. "Outside. I'm gonna kill you in the ravine out back." There was a slight crackling sound of spittle as the graybeard spread his lips in a smile.

He grabbed Longarm's Winchester and stepped back abruptly. "Get movin' now, or I'll drill you here! No one would care except maybe the grievin' widow yonder!" He scoffed.

Longarm glanced at the depot agent he'd first seen skulking outside the Wyoming Stage Company office when the lawman had first ridden into town. He'd seen the man again later, drinking with his cronies in the Dragoon Saloon.

"What got your long handles in a twist, old-timer?" Longarm asked, raising his hands shoulder-high as he turned toward the stairs.

"Shut up an' get movin'. On down the stairs and out the back door."

"All right, all right," Longarm said, moving slowly toward the stairs.

Now his own rifle was being pressed against his back. The old man reached forward and slid the lawman's Colt from its holster. "Just keep movin'. No funny moves. Best be sayin' a prayer, 'cause you're about to meet your maker. I'm sorry about this—truly I am. It ain't right, such a young, good-lookin' hombre havin' to meet his maker way before his time, but there just ain't no other way."

Longarm was descending the stairs. He glanced behind. The old man was following from about five steps up the staircase, just out of range if Longarm were to try wheeling on him to make a play for the rifle. Longarm's pistol was wedged behind the man's black belt and the waistband of his broadcloth trousers.

"No other way but to kill a federal lawman and feed his carcass to the coyotes, eh?" Longarm reached the second-floor landing and continued down the stairs toward the dark lobby below. "You did send that telegram—didn't you, old-timer?"

"That's right—I did," said the old man behind Longarm. He was breathing hard, nervous. "Didn't know what it was all about. Then someone up and kills Rainey an' I realized it wasn't nothin' I shoulda got mixed up in. Okay, I sent the damn telegram. Didn't know Rainey was dead till later, after I sent that note to your boss. Since I caused the problem, I reckon it's only fittin' I fix it."

As Longarm reached the bottom of the stairs, the old telegrapher said, "Turn to the left there. The back door's down the hall yonder. Dark in here but my eyesight's still keen. You try to make a move on me, I'll drill you with your own Winchester. Town'll thank me for it."

"Why would they thank you for it?"

Longarm reached the door. The curtain in the door's top pane was drawn over the glass, but murky light still washed through it. He saw the latch lever, tripped it, pushed the door open, and stepped out into the cool, late-summer morning.

Birds chirped and fluttered. Wood smoke perfumed the air. The sky was periwinkle blue, edged with gray. Thick shadows lingered out here behind the hotel.

"'Cause I'm about to prevent a whole passel o' trouble, that's why they'll thank me. Ain't none of your business, anyways. Never was, never would be the business of the federal government. Diamondback takes care of its own damn, busi—Ahhh, shit! Goddamn!"

Longarm had wheeled on the man as the old-timer had stumbled slightly on the doorjamb. The lawman had grabbed the Winchester's barrel and given it a hard jerk, ripping it free of the old telegrapher's grasp. Longarm turned the rifle maw-forward, rammed it against the old man's belly, and slid his Colt from behind the man's belt.

When he'd shoved the .44 into the holster on his own left hip, he took the old man's own pistol out of his coat pocket. It was an old Confederate-made, cap-and-ball revolver, rusty and badly scratched, its walnut grips held together with shrunken rawhide. Keeping his rifle barrel pressed against the old man's soft belly, Longarm held the telegrapher's gun up for a quick inspection, and chuckled.

"An old Leech and Rigdon. Haven't seen one o' these since the War of Northern Aggression."

"I carried it for the Star an' Bars," the old man croaked out, holding his hands high above his head and resting back against the hotel's rear wall. "Took a Yankee ball at Chickamauga. You gonna shoot me, now—with my own gun? I reckon I deserve it for bein' such a fool. Go ahead!"

Longarm lowered the Winchester and took it under his arm. He lowered the old Confederate pistol's loading lever, removed the cylinder with the nipples and balls, and stuffed it into his coat pocket. He flipped the gun in his hand and extended it to the old man, butt first.

"Now you can't hurt anybody with it. You'll get the wheel back when I leave here, though I ain't leavin' till I've run to ground the son of a bitch or sons of bitches who killed Sheriff Rainey."

Longarm set his rifle on his shoulder and opened the hotel door, about to head back inside. The old telegrapher gaped at him, holding his pistol low in his gnarled hand. "That's it?"

Longarm stopped. "It ain't it if you wanna tell me who killed Rainey."

The old man just stared at him, sheepish.

"Thought as much. Since you're too damn old to beat it out of, I reckon you're free to go."

"Des Rainey was my friend."

"You oughta help me seek justice for him, then."

"I can't." The old man shook his head and scrunched his eyes, genuinely grieved. "I just can't. I've got an old woman. Without me, she'd . . ." He shrugged and just wagged his head miserably.

"I understand," Longarm said, and went on inside the hotel.

He went back up to his room, washed the sex residue from his privates, grabbed his saddlebags and rifle, and headed back outside. Since it was still too early to hit the trail with the sheet of notepaper on which Meg had scratched out the route to the Garvey ranch, he headed over to Abigaile's for breakfast.

The same sexy young girl was there, sashaying around with her hips on fire. She was no friendlier this morning than she'd been the night before, but the breakfast she served him—a large stack of griddlecakes, two eggs, and a thick wedge of ham washed down with three mugs of piping black belly wash—padded him out nicely.

He lit a cheroot as he headed over to the livery barn to pick up his horse. Astride the bay, he rode over to the jailhouse for a look around the murder site. He doubted any clues as to who had shot Rainey remained in the office or in the street where Meg had watched her husband get blown—probably by a shotgun—but he wanted a look-see, just the same.

The sun was well up and spilling buttery gold light out of a clear, blue sky. Shopkeepers were out sweeping the dog and horse shit from their boardwalks, and the town's soaks were heading for the saloons for a red-eye.

Otherwise, Diamondback was still relatively quiet—only one farm wagon heading into town from the west, a wagon loaded with firewood heading in from the east, and two dogs sniffing around the high boardwalk beneath the Diamondback Mercantile, eagerly wagging their tails.

They probably had a cat or a skunk trapped under there, Longarm absently opined to himself.

The lawman tied the bay to the hitchrack fronting the sheriff's office, tripped the crude latch of the unlocked door, and went inside. He hadn't been looking around long—but long enough to satisfy himself that there were no clues there—when he heard near voices out in the street. He looked out the window over Rainey's desk to see four men angling toward the sheriff's office from the direction of the bank, which sat east of the Diamondback Hotel.

He recognized the dapper, bespectacled, well-dressed figure of the banker, Alexander Richmond, and the slouch-shouldered Dr. Baker, but the other two men Longarm had not seen before. One was young and also dressed in a crisp three-piece suit, while the fourth man was around Richmond's age—a tall, lean man in a black pinstripe suit with a gray bowler and a sweeping salt-and-pepper handlebar mustache.

Then Longarm remembered that he had seen the fourth gent before. He was the man Richmond had been talking with between the bank and the attorney's office when Longarm had fist ridden into town . . .

Longarm walked over to the door he'd left open and stepped out onto the front stoop, spreading his boots and hooking his thumbs behind his cartridge belt.

"Gentlemen, if you'd let me know you were coming, I'd have put the teapot on."

The four stopped in the street about ten feet out from the stoop.

"That's very funny, Marshal," Richmond said. "Very funny indeed. Here, I wanted to introduce you to some other citizens of Diamondback. The younker here is my son, Jack. That's Doc Baker to his left and Attorney Charles Mulligan on my right."

"How do you do, Marshal Long," said Richmond's son, a young, handsome man resembling his father in that his frame was nearly as compact, though his was broader through the chest and shoulders. He had thick, red-blond hair, freckles, and a spade-shaped chin to add some dimension to a heavy, handsome jaw. His goatee and mustache were well trimmed.

Longarm nodded to his morning visitors.

Richmond flourished a carved mahogany walking stick by its silver dancing-stallion handle. "Well, I suppose you've been snooping around long enough to have learned that Sheriff Rainey was killed right here."

"That's right."

The attorney, Mulligan, glanced owlishly at Richmond. "Rainey's wife told him, most likely." A blunt red nose marked the lawyer as a drinking man, as did the red-rimmed, red-veined, liquid-brown eyes on either side of it.

Richmond kept his disapproving gaze on Longarm. "Yes, I figured you'd run the poor woman down sooner or later, and bother her with your questions."

Longarm wondered if the men had any idea how long he'd been in Meg Rainey's room last night. He doubted anyone would have been able to see into her third-story windows, however. They most likely just assumed that since they were staying in the same hotel, they'd have run into each other.

"She didn't seem all that bothered," Longarm said.

Young Jack Richmond shook his head and furrowed his strawberry-blond brows beneath a wing of strawberry-blond hair hanging down over his left, pale blue eye. "You shouldn't have done that, Marshal. Mrs. Rainey . . . is a delicate creature, and she's been driven nearly mad by her husband's death."

"That's why she wants to find his killer," Longarm said, taking a puff off his cheroot and blowing the smoke over his visitors' heads. "And why you should want to find him, too."

Richmond drew a deep breath, expanding his chest and throwing his shoulders back. He glanced at the others around him, as though silently conferring, and then turned back to Longarm, jabbing the end of his walking stick at the ground before him.

"All right, Marshal, since you're so damn stubborn and won't leave this matter up to us, we've decided to tell you exactly what's been happening here. We want you to know that we thought—and continue to feel— that we came to our decision with the very best of intentions."

"Go on."

"We don't know who killed Rainey. We suspect a drifter who had a bone to pick with a lawman who once cost him some time behind bars, or possibly cost a friend the same. He was waiting here, shot Rainey, and fled. As simple as that."

"Since it's so simple, why didn't you tell me that before?"

Young Jack Richmond stepped forward, carefully adjusting the set of his bowler hat on his pretty blond curls. He had a hard, cold look in his eyes. "Because it was and still is our business. We will take care of the matter. We intend to hire a bounty hunter to run the killer to ground and bring him back here for punishment that will no doubt consist of his being hanged by his neck until he is dead. We owe Rainey that much. He was a good sheriff for a lot of years, and he dearly loved his wife."

"So you kept it quiet—you all and everyone else I've talked to in Diamondback have kept it quiet—because you want to hunt the killer yourselves. Or at least pay a bounty hunter to hunt him." Longarm laughed.

"That's the way it lays out, Marshal Long." This from Dr. Baker, who hadn't said anything until now. He had a nervous twitch that caused him to blink repeatedly. Unable to meet Longarm's gaze for more than a few seconds, he blinked and looked away, working his jaws like a cow chewing cud. "We'd just as soon you left our town now, sir. Leave this private, local matter to us and the rest of the citizens of Diamondback."

"It is not a federal matter," added Alexander Richmond. "And your presence has grown quite tiresome indeed. Now, will you please leave, or do I need to write a letter to your boss?"

"Keep your pen in your pocket, Mr. Mayor." Longarm sighed and looked around, feigning an air of defeat while trying not to imagine Billy Vail's response to such a missive and laugh.

He shrugged and returned his gaze to his four callers. "All right, if you wanna take care of your own sheriff's murder in your own way, and if the entire town is in agreement—hell, all right."

"What's that?" said Richmond.

Dr. Baker turned to Longarm, blinking rapidly and wrinkling the skin above the bridge of his nose. Mulligan scowled. Young Jack Richmond looked skeptical.

"I said have it your way. Never thought it would happen, but I do believe you people wore me down. And you're right, this ain't a federal matter. It's a local one."

Longarm took a last drag from his cheroot, tossed the stub in the street between the stoop and his four visitors, and hitched his cartridge belt higher on his lean hips. "It's all yours," he said, and walking down the porch steps, he canted his head toward the jailhouse. "Hope you find a new sheriff real soon. Every town needs a lawman."

Longarm untied the bay's reins from the hitchrack and stepped into the saddle. He backed the horse away from the sheriff's office, his four callers turning their heads to follow him.

To a man, they looked dubious. Mulligan's alcoholic nose turned a darker shade of red.

Longarm pinched his hat brim. "Luck to you."

He touched heels to the bay's flanks and sent the army remount galloping east along Diamondback's main street, heading for the open hills and the pass beyond the town. He did not, of course, reach those hills.

A quarter mile out of town, he stopped the bay and looked back toward Diamondback, which was obscured by wolf willows, rocky knolls, and sage. He could see no one moving about, which meant he was likely out of sight from town now, as well.

Quickly, he reined the bay south for another half a mile before turning the horse to follow Diamondback Creek nearly straight west, toward the Dan Garvey ranch and, hopefully, whatever problem had lured Sheriff Des Rainey out this way the day he was killed.

Chapter 14

The ranch headquarters was nestled along the north side of Diamondback Creek. A high sandstone ridge towered above it on the south side of the creek, which was lined with mixed conifers and aspens.

The Garvey Ranch announced itself by letters burned into the top crossbar of a timber portal straddling the trail leading into the place, and by a Box G brand burned into both ends of the crossbar. Longarm stopped the bay just inside the portal and looked around.

It had taken him an hour and a half to ride out here. Now at noon the sun blazed straight down on the low, gray, brush-roofed log cabin with a barn and corrals and a smaller cabin to the left, and two corrals to the right. A dog had come running out from the trees along the creek to stop in the middle of the yard and bark warningly at Longarm, glancing over its left shoulder at the cabin. It was a shaggy black-and-brown dog—probably a collie-shepherd mix. A man came out of the small cabin just beyond the barn to stare toward Longarm, a cup of coffee in his hand. He wore torn dungarees and suspenders, no hat.

It was noon and he was probably having lunch.

Just then the door of the main cabin opened. The man who'd opened it stayed back in the cabin's shadows for a time, so Longarm couldn't see much about him. The man reached to his left for a rifle. Cocking the rifle, he stepped out of the cabin and onto the narrow stoop fronting it. He glanced to his right, at the man standing in the doorway of the smaller cabin.

That was probably Garvey's hired hand, Calvin Johnson.

The man outside the main cabin, who was probably Garvey, stood in the middle of the stoop holding the rifle down low across his thighs, with casual threat. He canted his hatless head to one side as he stared toward Longarm.

The dog continued to bark. Inside the cabin behind Garvey, a baby was crying.

Longarm lightly touched heels to the bay's flanks, putting the horse forward. As he moved deeper into the yard, the dog barked louder, more angrily, though it moved only a few feet closer to Longarm and stopped, dutifully glancing over its shoulder toward the cabin to make sure its warning had been heard.

"Go lay down, Duke!" the man on the porch yelled.

The dog whimpered and, putting its head and tail down, strode back to the cabin and lay down near the bottom of the porch steps, continuing to stare toward Longarm.

The man whom Longarm assumed was Garvey came down the steps and stood by the dog. He was a lean, brown-haired man in suspenders, dungarees, and a spruce-green work shirt, the shirt's sleeves and white underwear sleeves rolled above his elbows.

"That's far enough," he told Longarm, and glanced at the hired man still standing, coffee cup in hand, in the bunkhouse's open doorway.

The lawman stopped the bay in the middle of the yard. "You Dan Garvey?"

"Who's askin'?"

"Custis Long. I'm a deputy U.S. marshal out of Denver. Rainey sent for me. I understand you're one of the last men—aside from his killer—to see him alive."

"Ah, shit!" Garvey said above the crying of the baby in the cabin behind him. "You're all I need!"

A woman holding a small child appeared in the cabin's doorway, atop the stoop. Around Garvey's age—late twenties, early thirties—she wore a plain gingham dress and an apron with frayed edges. The apron and the dress bulged over her pregnant belly.

"You know about Rainey, I take it?" Longarm said.

"Who in this county don't know what happened?" Garvey pointed an angry finger at Longarm. "You can just turn that horse around and ride the hell out of here. I don't know one damn thing about Rainey's killin'. I had nothin' to do with it! I don't know nothin' about it!"

"What did you want to see him about, Garvey?" Longarm slid his glance to the man standing in the bunkhouse doorway. "Why did you send your hired man into town to fetch him? That's all I want to know."

"Get out of here, goddamnit"—Garvey lifted his gaze

to peer warily around behind Longarm—"before they see ya out here and get me an' my family in trouble."

"Why would you be in any trouble?"

Garvey just stared at Longarm, as did the woman and the hired man.

Longarm decided to play another card. "His wife sent me, Garvey. She wants to know who killed her husband. Can't blame her—wantin' to know that. Your wife would want to know."

Garvey pinched his eyes and opened his mouth to snap angrily back, but then the woman said something too quietly for Longarm to hear. Garvey closed his mouth and stood scowling at the stranger sitting the bay in his yard. Finally, the rancher rested his rifle on his shoulder and walked out away from the cabin, heading toward Longarm.

The dog rose and followed him slowly, tentatively, from five feet back, working its nose and lifting its bushy black-and-brown tail.

"Look," Garvey said, "I want no part of none of that. I got a wife and a kid, and Sarah's in the family way. I got a ranch to run. I can't get in no trouble with them fellas in town."

Longarm swung down from the saddle. He wanted to put himself on even footing, smooth the rancher's feathers. "What kind of trouble?"

"What they done . . . over there at the Bear-Runner Place." Garvey lifted his chin to indicate east. "They was good folks and they didn't deserve what happened to 'em. That's why I fetched the sheriff. But those men in town, an' Tanner Webster—they killed him because they thought he was gonna cause a stink over it."

"Who're the Bear-Runners?"

Garvey glanced over his shoulder at his wife, who seemed to encourage him with her eyes, gently jouncing the child in her arms. The hired hand shuttled his skeptical gaze between Longarm and Garvey.

"Injun family back down the creek the way you came. About two miles. Someone shot 'em, killed 'em, burned their cabin. Hanged one of the boys—George."

"Why?"

Garvey looked around as though worried someone else were hearing. He scanned Longarm's backtrail and then looked toward the north.

The rancher ran a nervous hand across his mouth. "I think maybe Tanner's lost some cattle and he just naturally figured the Bear-Runner boys had collared 'em, maybe sold 'em up on the Wind River Reservation. That's where most of the rustled beef ends up around here. The price of rustlin' out here, especially if the rustlers is Injuns or even half-breeds, is just what happened to them."

Garvey shook his head, looking down, a pained, angry look in his eyes. "I don't like it. No, sir. Bear-Runner's family—they was good folks. Them boys was quiet, but if they was gonna collar beef, hell, they'd have collared mine. And I haven't lost no beef to nothin' but winter snows and coyotes and bullberry thickets in the three years since the Bear-Runners moved in down the creek. They cut firewood for me, gave me a good price for it. And when they shot a deer on my land, they always left a quarter of the carcass on my doorstep. No, sir—I think Tanner was barkin' up the wrong tree and them poor Bear-Runners paid the price for it."

He threw up an angry arm and jutting finger. "But don't you tell no one I said that. You do, and I'll call you a bald-faced liar!"

He paused and then added, as he rubbed the back of his hand across his mouth again and turned to stare north, "Me an' Rainey buried 'em. Someone bushwhacked us. We didn't get a good look at who it was. Maybe one of Tanner's men, maybe one of Richmond's. But the same shooter must've killed Rainey when he got back to town."

"What does Richmond have to do with Tanner?"

"They're in business together. Hell, this is a small town. All the mucky-mucks stick together. The ruination of one could mean the ruin of all of 'em. It's sort of an unwritten rule in this town, ever since Tanner and Richmond set up the bank and then Mulligan came in from back East to run his law practice. He's Tanner Webster's brother-in-law."

"What's the sawbones got to do with it?"

Garvey hiked a shoulder. "Nothin'. He's just the third man on the town council's all. Richmond, both Alexander an' his son Jack, runs things around here. Them an' Mulligan and Tanner Webster."

"And you think Tanner killed the Bear-Runners, and the rest of the town is protecting him because he's rich."

Garvey laughed mirthlessly. "Yeah, that's what I think! He goes out of business, the whole town suffers."

"Where will I find Tanner?"

"North. Straight north about six miles. But I wouldn't ride out there, if I was you. You ain't got no friends here, Marshal. You ride up there, you'll disappear and no one'll ever hear from you again. Rainey an' the Bear-Runners—they're dead. It ain't right, but that's how it is. Me? I got my family to think about. I don't know if you're a family man, but even if you ain't, you got your own neck to think about."

Garvey turned to share a look with his hired hand. "I'd think about it, if I was you. And I'd ride back to Denver and forget you ever heard of Diamondback."

"And what'll I tell Rainey's widow?"

"Tell her he's dead an' buried. We all gotta die. The livin' folks—they gotta move on." Garvey started to turn away, but then he stopped and said, "It's just like what happened two years ago out east. No sense in it."

"What happened out east?"

"In the next valley over, a family was murdered. A whole family—prospectin' family with a purty young daughter—burned alive in their cabin." Garvey shook his head. "It's just like that craziness over there. It's a cryin' shame. There ain't no sense in none of it, but there it is."

Shrugging, the rancher turned and strode back toward the cabin, the dog growling softly at Longarm and then turning to follow its master.

Garvey's wife walked out away from the cabin and stopped at the top of the porch steps. "Mister!" she called. "You tell Meg Rainey that just as soon as our second one is born, I'll ride to town to see her. I know she needs a friend, and I'll be in to visit with her before the winter. I'll bring her a cake!"

Longarm pinched his hat brim. "I'll tell her, Mrs. Garvey!"

Longarm swung up onto the bay's back and trotted out under the ranch portal. He knew that Mrs. Garvey meant well, but Meg Rainey needed more than a cake. And Longarm was going to get it for her before he'd even consider leaving Diamondback.

Of course, the attempt might get him killed, with the number of men he suddenly found himself up against. When he got back to Diamondback, he'd send a telegram to Billy Vail and request a little help . . .

The thought hadn't finished passing through his mind before he gave an ironic chuff. Wasn't that just what Rainey had done before that shotgun blast had blown him out of his office and into the street?

Longarm glanced north, toward the Webster Ranch, and considered all that Garvey had told him. He'd have to visit the place sooner or later, but first he'd check out the Bear-Runner Ranch. The killers' trail was likely cold by now, but Longarm still felt compelled to visit the place where all the trouble had started, the place that Rainey had visited just before he was murdered.

He swung off the trail and followed a game trail that hugged the creek. It was shady here, the warm breeze rattling the cottonwood and aspen leaves. Longarm paused to let the bay drink from a small, dark pool pushing up against the low bank, and then he rode on, following the gently meandering creek along the base of the steep southern ridge.

He'd been in some tight spots before, but this was a kicker.

About forty-five minutes after he'd set out from the Garvey Ranch, he rode up to the edge of the Bear-

Runner place. He recognized it by the cabin and barn, both heaps of burned and half-burned logs encircling separate messes of more burned and charred heaps of furnishings.

He rode around the cabin one time and then he rode around the barn. He wasn't looking for anything in particular. The killer or killer's trail was cold. He was just riding and thinking about what to do next.

He saw the four graves mounded near the creek, and rode over and swung down from the bay's back. He removed his hat and stared at the mounded dirt and rocks. Coyotes had been poking around the graves, trying to burrow in. But Rainey and Garvey had buried the Bear-Runners well. The carrion-eaters hadn't dug down to the bodies.

Longarm looked around at the creek and at the burned cabin and barn and then at the corrals. A forlorn feeling came over him. He hadn't known the Bear-Runners, of course, but Garvey had told him a little. Longarm had the sense of a family at work here. A family at odds with most other folks in the county, including the people of Diamondback, because their skin had been a darker cast.

Whatever the color of their skin, they'd been a family, and they'd obviously worked hard together. They'd no doubt loved one another in the way that most families did, helping one another through the hard task of surviving in a place this remote. There was an air of industry and goodness here in the way that the Bear-Runners, a family of outsiders, had built this humble ranch along this quiet creek.

A ranch that someone had burned, the same

someone who'd killed everyone in the family. The killer likely thought he could get away with what he'd done because the Bear-Runners were Indians and half-breeds. Who would care?

Longarm had no idea if there'd been any rustling or not. The injustice of the savage attack set a fire in his loins. Fanning the flames was his knowledge that he very likely would never be able to run the killer, or killers, to ground.

The odds were against him. A powerful rancher. A town. A county. The whole matter enswathed in secrecy nourished by powerful white men . . .

Longarm had been sitting on a log by the creek, the bay standing in the trees nearby, cropping grass. Now, intending to head to town and send that telegram to Billy Vail, he rose from the log and turned toward the horse.

A rifle cracked loudly. The bullet plowed into the log where Longarm had been sitting.

Longarm froze, then turned toward the cabin. The bearded gent he'd beat the shit out of in the Dragoon Saloon stepped out from behind the cabin, a rifle in his hands. He wore a bandage around the top of his head. Another, heavier bandage—and a neck brace—encircled his neck.

A second man stepped out from the cabin's opposite corner, to the bearded man's left. He wore a black hat and a cream duster.

This was the mustached gent, whose face was a blaze of purple around the white bandage splayed across his nose.

The mustached gent was aiming a rifle straight out from his shoulder at Longarm, angrily barking, "Go ahead and pull that hogleg, you son of a bitch! Do it! Please, do it! I got me an' itch that needs scratchin' real bad!"

Chapter 15

Both the bearded gent and the mustached gent stared down their rifles at Longarm. The lawman glanced at his bay in the trees nearby. More specifically, he glanced at his rifle sheathed on the bay's right side.

The rifle was just then being slid from the scabbard by a man in a cream shirt, suspenders, and a billowy red neckerchief. He had another rifle in his right hand, aimed at Longarm from the man's right hip.

The man grinned, fresh chaw dribbling down from one corner of his mouth. Two other men stood in the trees around him, both tough nuts armed with rifles, one or two pistols holstered on their hips. All three wore chaps, which marked them as range riders.

Tanner Webster's men?

"Lookin' for this?" said the man holding Longarm's rifle.

Longarm felt a cold stone drop in his belly as he watched the three men in chaps walk toward him from along the creek. As they did, another man stepped out from behind a tree near the water and walked toward Longarm. He was lighting a fat cigar, but when he lowered his cupped hands from his face, blowing smoke, Longarm saw the wedge-shaped, dark red nose of the Diamondback attorney, Charles Mulligan.

Mulligan puffed the stogie, smoke billowing around his glowering craggy ruin of an alcoholic face and the black bowler hat tipped back off his forehead. As the three ranch hands approached Longarm, the two others moved out from the cabin, squinting malevolently down their rifle barrels, keeping the long guns aimed at the lawman's head.

Longarm held his hands waist high, palms out, mind racing to find a way out of his current predicament, but it didn't look good. Not good at all.

Should have sent that note to Billy before he'd ridden out here. Too late now.

"Well, well, Mulligan," Longarm said. "You ride out here to admire your handiwork?"

The three men in chaps stopped about ten feet away from Longarm, between him and the creek. The other two men, with the swollen faces and glowing bandages, stopped just on the other side of the graves, aiming their rifles as though wanting desperately to trigger them. Mulligan stopped about six feet back from the men wearing chaps.

The lawyer shook his head slowly. "You should have gone on back to Denver, like you said you were gonna do. I knew you weren't, though. I knew where you'd head, sooner or later. Just so happens Tanner had three men in town today. Tanner's good about hirin' his men out for . . . special duties above and beyond the call of Webster's own brand, you might say."

The lawyer smiled smugly.

"Just like the other two in town, eh? The two that got sent to their reward last night."

"Mr. Webster didn't take kindly to that, Mr. Lawman," said the man who had Longarm's rifle resting on his shoulder.

"I'll apologize when I see him."

"Oh, you're not gonna have the honor of meeting Mr. Webster," said Mulligan. "In fact, you won't be meeting anyone else . . . ever again. This is the end of your trail." He shook his head, appearing genuinely frustrated. "Why couldn't you be convinced that this was too much for you? Why didn't you just go back to Denver and forget you'd ever heard of Diamondback?"

Longarm sighed. "I reckon I just don't like to believe that anything's too much for me. The stubborn sort, I reckon. But now I see that I chewed way too big a bite out of that apple. I sure did." The longer he talked, the more time he figured he was buying—for what, he wasn't sure.

"You sure did."

"So, who the hell's responsible for this, Mulligan?" Longarm glanced at the graves and hardened his jaws. "Four dead people—a family—their cabin burned . . ."

"Nasty business, isn't it?" The attorney removed his hat and ran his hand back through the four or five strands of coarse, sandy-gray hair on his liver-spotted head. "I'm afraid the entire family simply had to suffer for young George's transgression."

"And what transgression was that?"

Mulligan stepped broadly around Longarm and stared down at the graves, a distasteful look on his craggy face. "The boy wouldn't leave my daughter alone. I rode out here with Sheriff Rainey one day, asked Bear-Runner myself to keep George from coming to town. He and my daughter—they were sneaking around behind my back. Bear-Runner refused to do anything about it, said it was none of our business. And then . . . Louise ended up in the family way."

Longarm stared. When he was sure he'd actually heard what he thought he'd heard, he hung his lower jaw in shock. It took him a moment to get the words out. "You mean . . . to tell me . . . that you had this whole family . . . murdered . . . because their son and your daughter were in love?"

"The boy was a savage," Mulligan snapped. "He . . . they wouldn't listen to me. I, Louise's father. This could have been avoided but neither one would listen to reason. I had to have her sent away." He wrung his hands together as he continued to glare down at the graves. "Her mother and her aunt took her to Santa Fe . . . to see a doctor . . ."

"Christ!" Seething, Longarm balled his fists at his sides. It took every ounce of effort to keep from belting the old bastard. "You're crazy, Mulligan. And you're a cold-blooded killer."

"You're obviously not a father."

"Who did you have to burn the cabin—these two?" Longarm looked at the two men whose faces he'd rearranged and who had lowered their rifles slightly, keeping them aimed at the lawman's belly. They stood on the other side of the graves, looking eager as trained attack dogs.

"Lonigan and Muehler—that's right. They work for Richmond. He lent them to me for this special favor. They had no problem with killing savages, did you, boys?"

"Hell, no," said the bearded hombre—Lonigan. "As long as the pay's right, we'll take care of any problem, large or small. That includes killin' us a federal lawman."

"Be right satisfyin'," added Muehler, whose broken nose apparently required that he breathe through his mouth.

Longarm turned back to Mulligan. "So Rainey found out about the killings out here, and . . ."

"He would not have listened to reason," Mulligan said. "He'd been in agreement with old Bear-Runner about this being none of my business."

"And you had him killed."

"Oh, I didn't." Mulligan shifted his curious gaze between Lonigan and Muehler. "I assume Richmond did, knowing that Rainey would come after me. Rainey could be a stubborn old cuss. It was no secret he had a soft spot for the Bear-Runners. He'd been ignoring Tanner Webster's complaints about their rustling for the past two years."

The attorney held his cigar out and tapped ashes onto one of the graves. "Richmond and I share half interests in the bank as well as in the Dragoon Saloon. If one of us went down, we'd both go down."

Lonigan glanced at Muehler, shrugged. "Whoever killed Rainey, it wasn't me."

"Me, neither," Muehler said, also shrugging. "Richmond never told me to do nothin' regardin' Rainey."

Longarm glanced at Tanner's three cowhands. They all shrugged, shook their heads. "We wasn't given no orders to kill the Bear-Runners," the tallest of the three said, one leg cocked forward, boot heel resting casually atop a rock. "But Mr. Tanner sure didn't weep when he heard the news."

Longarm looked at Mulligan. The man had no reason to lie, and neither did the others. As far as they were concerned, Longarm wouldn't be riding off the Bear-Runner ranch alive.

If none of these men had killed the sheriff, who did?

Longarm knew that the odds were stacked against him ever finding out.

"What do you want us to do with him, Mr. Mulligan?" asked Muehler.

"What do you think I want you to do?" Mulligan said, staring at Longarm with an amused expression, blowing smoke out his nostrils. "Shoot him. We'll haul him away and stow him where no one will ever find him—except for the carrion-eaters, that is. They gotta eat, too—don't they, Deputy Long? Then we'll ride over and talk to Dan Garvey about how I don't appreciate him talkin' to strangers."

Longarm still had his fists and jaws clenched. "You're one sick son of a bitch, Mulligan."

"Mind if we take our time with him?" This from Lonigan, wincing as he adjusted the heavy brace around his neck. "Doc says I'm gonna be wearin' this for the next two months. I'd like to get a little satisfaction for the pain."

"Sure, sure," Mulligan said, puffing the cigar and grinning wickedly, narrowing both eyes. "Why not? Might be fun. Best take his hogleg first. This federal boy ain't likely to fight fair."

Lonigan glared at Longarm, thrusting his rifle out belligerently. "Raise them hands high and keep 'em raised."

Facing the bearded hard case, Longarm raised his hands to his shoulders.

"Higher!"

Longarm raised his hands above his head. He stared at Lonigan, who said to Muehler out the side of his mouth, "Watch him, now," and stepped up close to Longarm, crouching over his rifle. When he was within two feet of the lawman, Lonigan removed his left hand from his rifle and reached toward Longarm.

When he'd wrapped that hand around the handle of the lawman's holstered .44 and started to pull, Longarm, having nothing to lose, slashed his right fist down hard against Lonigan's right arm. The rifle discharged into the ground between the two men.

Longarm lunged forward and drove his right knee into the big man's crotch.

As Lonigan screamed and folded like a jackknife, Longarm drove his other knee into the man's forehead. Longigan flew backward, limbs akimbo, and ran into Mulligan, who gave a howl and twisted around and stumbled backward.

The two men fell together, Lonigan atop Mulligan. Longarm reached for the rifle lying near Lonigan. He'd just gotten one hand around the breech and started to pull it up off the ground, when Muehler rammed the butt of his rifle against the back of Longarm's head.

Red lights flashed in Longarm's eyes, and he released the rifle, stumbling forward and dropping to his hands and knees. Hammering agony screeched through his skull, setting up a tolling in his ears. He felt blood ooze through the hot gash the mustached hard case had opened in the back of his head, about six inches up from his neck.

Beneath the tolling in his ears, he heard Mulligan groan loudly, bellowing, "Oh, oh! I think you broke my leg you big lummox!"

Lonigan rolled to one side, groaning and covering his crotch with his big hands. Longarm saw a shadow slide over him, and he was about to roll over to face Muehler, who Longarm could tell by the man's shadow was about to ram the rifle butt against his head again.

"No!" Mulligan pointed warningly at Muehler. "Don't kill him. Oh, no! Not yet!" He was sitting on the ground, leaning back and stretching his lips back from his teeth. His leg was bent oddly at the knee.

"You all right, Mr. Mulligan?" asked one of the Tanner men.

"Do I look all right, you fool!" Mulligan drew a deep breath, groaned again, and threw his arms toward the Tanner men. "One of you take my arms. Another, grab my right foot, and pull. Knee—it's out of the socket. Gotta jerk it back in!"

Longarm rolled onto a hip and shoulder. He felt sick and dizzy from the clubbing, but he didn't think he'd lose consciousness. As he waited for the searing pain in his head to pass, he watched one of the Tanner men grab Mulligan under the arms and another grab his right foot. One man pulled one way while the other pulled the opposite way. There was a snicking, a wooden grinding sound, and when the one hand released the attorney's foot, the leg was straight again.

Mulligan flopped on the ground, panting like a landed fish, red-faced and sweating.

After a few minutes, the hard cases forming a circle around the attorney and Longarm, Mulligan cast his fiery-eyed gaze at the lawman. "Someone get a rope."

"Gonna hang him?" asked one of the Tanner men.

Mulligan shook his head. "Dutch ride!" He snickered evilly, then winced and grabbed his knee.

Chapter 16

"Dutch ride" was a ranch term for dragging a man behind a horse.

Longarm had endured Dutch rides before, but he hadn't liked them much. Most times, they meant a slow, violent, and agonized death. For him, because he'd been lucky, they'd only cost him a set of torn clothes and sundry scrapes, bruises, and thorn pricks.

But in most cases, they were fatal, as in most cases they were intended to be.

This one, of course, was intended to be fatal, as well. It was a neat trick. Longarm wouldn't mind treating Mulligan to it, but at the moment, with four rifles aimed at his head from six feet away in all directions, he could only sit there by the graves of the Bear-Runner family and wait for the third Tanner man to fetch his horse and riata.

Mulligan sat back against a tree, injured leg stretched out before him, the other one curled beneath it. He glared at Longarm, mopping sweat from his forehead and brow.

"That knee's gonna grieve me somethin' terrible for a long time to come, you son of a bitch," he groused.

"You don't know how sorry I am." Longarm grinned and got a boot in his ribs for his efforts.

The blow rolled him onto his back, where he lay gasping. The bearded Lonigan glared down at him. "That's for the knee in my balls, you bastard!"

Mulligan said, "Turn your horns in, Lonigan. He's about to pay . . . in the worst way imaginable."

As though in support of the attorney's statement, hooves thumped on the far side of the creek. Longarm turned his head to see one of the Tanner men gallop across the creek, water splashing golden in the late-day sun.

Whacking his buckskin across the ass with a coiled riata, the rider—a tall man with a black, funnel-brimmed hat, red checked shirt, brown chaps, and green neckerchief—gave a triumphant whoop and came up the gentle slope and checked the buckskin down hard.

Dust wafted over Longarm. The horse shook its head and blew.

As the rider uncoiled the riata, shaking out a loop, Longarm felt a wicked intensity flood his veins. He had to make a move now—any move—or his chances for survival were slimmer than they'd been so far this afternoon.

He heaved himself to his feet, intending to grab for one of the rifles, but the braining he'd taken him had upset his balance. He stumbled.

Lonigan and Muehler grabbed him from behind and held him as the rider expertly cast his broad loop straight out over the buckskin's head. While Muehler pinned Longarm's arms behind his back, Lonigan caught the loop and jerked it down over Longarm's head and shoulders.

The rider backed the ranch horse up two feet, drawing the loop taut and pinning the lawman's arms to his sides. He backed the horse up again, more sharply, and Longarm flew forward off his feet and, unable to break his fall, hit the ground on his face with a grunt.

"Tie his hands!" shouted the rider, wide-eyed with glee. He was really going to have a good time now, giving a federal lawman a Dutch ride over rocks and cacti!

When one of the others had used a three-foot length of rope to tie Longarm's wrists together in front of him, and adjust the loop under his arms, Mulligan shouted, "Show him a real good time, now, Rance!"

Rance whooped and ground his spurs into the buckskin's flanks. Longarm grunted as his tied hands were jerked straight up above his shoulders. The rope under his arms cut into his armpits, and he was nearly pulled out of his boots as he shot forward behind the galloping buckskin.

He was dragged down the slope, bouncing and twisting and turning, and into the stream. The rocks of the streambed hammered every bone in his body. One smashed against the side of his head. A pointed one rammed against his breastbone, sending fiery lances of agony all through him.

The buckskin galloped up the opposite bank, and

Longarm followed, soaked and bruised and bloody, at
the mercy of horse and rider. As they cut through the
trees, it was softer going in the grass. Out on the open
ground, the clumps of sage and occasional rocks beat
against him, dirt clods and dust from the buckskin's
hammering hooves pelting him.

Longarm put his head down, heard the grunts and
groans being pounded out of him as he bounced along
behind the whooping rider. He tried desperately,
futilely, to free his hands, but the rope binding his
wrists was too tight. He felt as though the rope under
his arms was going to rip his shoulders from their
sockets.

There was a moment's reprieve as the whooping
rider slowed the buckskin and swung it around. Longarm had come to a rolling stop. Now, dirty and
muddy, his shirt, coat, and pants torn, he scrambled
up onto his knees, fighting madly against the ropes
binding his hands and trying to shrug out from beneath
the loop.

He saw the black-hatted rider, Rance, whipping his
rein ends against the buckskin's flanks as the horse
whinnied, lunged off its rear hooves, and galloped hard
back in the direction from which it had come, racing
toward the trees and the creek and the men waiting by
the graves. Longarm watched the rope lying on the
ground before him and then steeled himself as it jerked
taut.

He cursed sharply as he was pulled up and forward,
his jaws slamming together, his chest and belly hammering the ground before he was jerked up again and
forward, racing along about fifteen feet behind the

buckskin's scissoring hooves and arched tail. Brush and cacti raked him raw. He bounced off rocks and then, as they approached the creek, he careened off several trees.

The creek was a quick bath, but he was promptly dirty and muddy again as Rance and the buckskin lurched him up the opposite bank. To his right, the other men stood whooping and hollering and waving their hats or their arms. Mulligan leaned against the tree, head back, mouth drawn wide as he laughed. Rance glanced back at Longarm and smiled, showing a line of dirty yellow teeth between his lips.

Longarm squinted his eyes against the dirt clods and broken weeds flying at him. All he could do was give himself over to it. Fighting didn't help. The horse would have to stop again. He hoped he was still conscious when it did, because he had to try something, anything.

He was glad when, looking up from beneath his dust-caked brows, he saw the buckskin slow and begin to turn. Rance was swinging it back around.

Hope was a feeble flame inside the beaten and bloody lawman. It grew a little larger when he saw an egg-shaped rock to his right. It was about four feet high, a little larger around than Longarm's own waist. He hoped it was well planted in the ground.

Longarm heaved himself to his torn and bloody knees and then his feet. As the rider whooped and slapped his hat against the buckskin's right hip, laughing and lunging once more toward the creek, Longarm ran around the rock one and a half times. The rope had just been drawn taut around the rock when

Longarm dropped to a knee and shoved a shoulder hard against the stone, on the side opposite the creek.

He stared at the rope hugging the rock. It quivered, scraped dust and bits of dried moss from the rock. The horse gave a shrill whinny. Rance screamed. There was a loud thump and the violent rattle of a bridle chain.

Longarm looked over the rock to see the horse lying on its side atop Rance, who struggled to regain its feet. Dust billowed and wafted. The horse's saddle hung down the buckskin's right side. Rance was screaming and flopping his arms as the horse ground its rear hooves into Rance's belly and groin as it struggled back to all four feet.

Longarm lunged to a standing position and ran, stumbling, one and a half times around the rock, in the opposite direction from before. He ran toward where the horse stood by the rider flopping and mewling on the ground, in the dust cloud still billowing around him and the horse. The buckskin shook itself and looked down at Rance and then at the man running toward it.

"Don't run," Longarm urged through gritted teeth, watching the other end of the rope where it was dallied around the saddle hanging down the horse's side.

But then the horse did run. The slack jerked out of the rope, and Longarm flew forward and braced himself for another hard ride. But then the gods smiled. The horse shook free of the saddle, and the saddle dropped to the ground about six feet beyond the bellowing Rance.

Longarm let the slack rope drop to his feet, and he

stepped out of it. He ran over to the rider, who was trying to draw his pistol as he writhed, his anxious gaze on Longarm. The lawman kicked the gun out of Rance's hand and then rammed his boot hard into Rance's right side, rolling him over.

"Stop!" the man screamed. "I think my legs are broken!"

"That's a cryin' shame," Longarm raked out, dropping to his knees and shoving both hands toward his left pocket, where he kept his folding barlow knife.

As he awkwardly shoved a hand into the pocket, he cast his gaze back toward the creek. The other men were running toward him. He could see their hatted heads jouncing just below the lip of the slope. They were about eighty yards away, moving fast and yelling.

Longarm slid the knife out of his pocket. He opened it, took the handle in his right hand, and angled the blade across his palm and onto the rope between his wrists. Using only the thumb and index finger of his right hand, he began to jerk the blade against the rope. He cast another nervous gaze toward the creek.

The four other men aside from Mulligan were running toward him, holding their rifles up high across their chests. They ran abreast, about six feet apart. As one stopped and raised his rifle to his shoulder, Longarm felt the rope between his wrists slacken slightly as the blade sliced through two strands.

He heard the whine of the bullet as it zipped past his right ear and then thumped into the ground behind him. A half second later, the crack of the rifle reached his ears.

Longarm threw himself forward, using the writhing man before him as marginal cover, and continued to saw desperately at the rope between his wrists.

Rifles cracked. Slugs plumed dirt around him, spanged off rocks, snapped sage branches. One seared across his left shoulder, mostly tearing his coat. Another made a near wet, cracking sound, and Rance stopped writhing.

Longarm looked at him and saw a fist-sized exit hole on the near side of Rance's head oozing brains and liver-colored blood.

The knife cut through the last rope strand, and Longarm's wrists came free. As the shooters continued running toward him, fanning out as they came, he made a mad dash to the dead man's saddle and slipped Rance's carbine from its scabbard. Pumping a cartridge into the chamber, he swung around and ran toward the rock behind him. A slug carved a shallow trough across the back of his left thigh, setting up a burning in his leg.

Another slug hammered the rock as he dropped behind it. Another thumped into the ground an inch beyond the toe of his right boot.

The shooters were moving too fast, and they were too anxious, for accurate shooting. They were near enough now that Longarm could hear their foot thuds and spur chings.

"Get around him, Lonigan—all the way right!" shouted Muehler. "I'll swing left!"

As soon as they got around him, they'd have him.

Time to make his move.

Longarm pushed off the rock and swung to his left,

dropping to his left knee and firing the Winchester twice quickly, his first shot hammering the dead center of Lonigan's chest. His second shot had missed the man running behind Lonigan by a hair, but it had forced the man to stop and drop to a knee.

Longarm pumped and fired, painting a dark circle in the nub of the man's right cheek. The other two shooters—Muehler and the third Tanner rider—had been taken by surprise. They shouted and swung toward Longarm, but neither got off another shot before Longarm's dancing, smoking carbine sent them stumbling straight back and down, where they both flopped as the blood pumped out of them.

A heavy, dark wave of fatigue washed over Longarm. He dropped as though he'd been felled by a sledgehammer, and lay on his back, catching his breath. After he caught it, he continued to lie there. Muehler was moaning and groaning, but his moans and groans grew gradually quieter.

After about twenty minutes, they stopped altogether.

Longarm dozed, every bone, muscle, and tendon in his body calling out for mercy. His clothes hung on him in tatters. His bloody knees and elbows shone where his sleeves and pants had been entirely ripped away. His lips were cut. One eye was swollen partly shut.

But he had one more man to see to.

Then he'd head for Diamondback to continue the investigation, though in his current condition the idea felt like an anvil on his shoulders. So far, he'd found out who'd killed the Bear-Runner family and why, but he had no idea who'd killed Sheriff Rainey, and that's what he'd been sent out here to find out in the first place.

It had to have been Richmond. Had to.

The battered lawman heaved a weary sigh as he stepped around the body of the man who'd dragged him half to death, and made his way down the gradual slope toward the creek and, he hoped, Mulligan.

Chapter 17

As Longarm walked down the slope toward the creek, he saw Mulligan sitting by the tree, back erect, nervous eyes staring at the bedraggled man walking toward him. The attorney blinked, incredulous, and then, realizing that Longarm was the only one walking out of the dustup alive, he gave a startled, enraged bellow and began struggling to unsheath the pistol on his hip.

Longarm stopped, raised the carbine, which he'd reloaded from the cartridges on his own belt, aimed, and fired. The slug slapped the attorney back against the tree. The man looked startled. He dropped the pistol he'd just clawed from its holster, and looked at his right arm.

He gave another bellowing cry, rolled to his left, his wounded arm hanging uselessly at his side, and began to crawl wildly, awkwardly down the slope toward the creek.

Longarm walked over to his bay standing a ways

upstream and fished a set of handcuffs and a set of leg irons from his saddlebags. He led the bay over to where Mulligan was trying to fight his way on his hands across the stream, yelling, and the lawman tied the bay's reins to a branch. He walked into the stream and planted a boot on the attorney's ass. He drove Mulligan forward into the two-foot-deep stream and then cuffed his hands behind his back.

The man was helpless, in miserable pain. All he could do was curse and berate Longarm almost incoherently as Longarm closed the shackles around his ankles.

Longarm turned and walked back up onto the bank. Behind him, Mulligan slumped back in the water, shouting, "I need a doctor!"

"Tomorrow," Longarm said without turning around. "We'll be spending the night here."

"Help me, you son of a bitch!" Mulligan shouted. "You can't leave me trussed up out here in this cold water!"

Longarm pulled his Maryland rye bottle out of his saddlebags and took a long, pain-stemming pull. "Can't I?"

When he figured the attorney had taken a long enough bath, Longarm hauled him out of the stream and tied him to a tree. He wrapped a neckerchief around the man's wounded arm so he wouldn't bleed to death, cheating the hangman. Then the lawman cleaned his many scrapes and abrasions in the stream before building a large fire and suppering on beef jerky, coffee, and rye.

He shared with Mulligan no more of the grub than a single strip of jerky and some creek water. The way Longarm saw it, the cold-blooded killer deserved merely enough nourishment to sustain him until he could hang. Mulligan complained vociferously but not at length.

Apparently, the attorney wasn't fond of the idea of spending the night with a rock stuffed in his mouth and secured behind a knotted neckerchief.

After good dark, Longarm built up the fire, finished his bottle, tossed the empty at Mulligan, and then rolled up in his blankets. He slept like a dead man until well after dawn.

He built up the fire again, made coffee, sharing half a cup and a single jerky strip with the attorney, who was weakened from blood loss, and then saddled the bay and Mulligan's white-socked black. He removed the attorney's leg irons, helped him into the saddle, and tied his hands to the horn.

Mulligan looked gaunt and pale. Longarm didn't care.

Longarm kept the pace slow as he and Mulligan headed east. The sun climbed, raining heat. Mid-morning, Longarm caught a slight flicker of movement off to his right, around the base of a small, cone-shaped butte. He reined the bay to a sudden stop. Good thing he did, because he otherwise would have ridden headfirst into the bullet that sang past his face to plunk into the bluff standing off the trail on his left.

The rifle's crack echoed a second later.

"Oh, Lord!" screamed Mulligan, sagging in his saddle. "Oh, Lord—now what the hell is going on?"

As another slug spanged off a rock several feet short of the trail, the attorney shouted weakly, "Stop shooting, you fools! It's Mulligan! Stop shooting this instant!"

The lawyer's voice cracked.

Longarm had swung down from his saddle as quickly as he could in his tender condition, and dropped to a knee in the trail. He aimed at where he'd seen the movement and the brief smoke plume, and fired two quick shots. Then he saw a figure scramble up the side of the bluff several feet, and disappear around its eastern shoulder.

Quickly, he tied Mulligan's horse to a shrub beside the trail. He swung up onto the bay's back. He ground his heels into the horse's flanks and bounded off across the flat between the trail and the bluff, slanting toward the position from which the dry-gulcher had been shooting.

His heart hammered eagerly. He was beaten to a frazzle, but hope yawned in him. Maybe he finally had Rainey's killer . . .

He closed the hundred-yard stretch of ground and leaped from the bay's back near the bluff's rocky base. He dropped to a knee, racking a shell into his Winchester's breech and aiming toward the eastern shoulder.

No movement.

No sounds.

Then there was the rataplan of distant hoofbeats.

Longarm bounded off his heels, ran up the side of the bluff, and peered off its eastern slope. A rider in a cream shirt and brown vest was galloping away toward

some trees and another bluff a hundred yards south-
east. Longarm cursed, raised his rifle, drew a bead on
the man's back. He held fire as the rider bounded into
the trees and around the far side of the bluff, gone.

Longarm cursed. He'd been too far away to get a
good look at the man. All he knew was that the bushwhacker wore a cream shirt, a brown vest, and a cream
hat. The horse was a nondescript dun.

There was no use trying to follow him. Whoever it
was likely knew this country better than Longarm did
and would be almost impossible to find before night-
fall. Besides, Longarm had Mulligan to throw in jail.

He rode back to the trail, to find Mulligan where
he'd left him, sitting slump-shouldered in his saddle.
The attorney wagged his head, crestfallen. "I declare,
you got more lives than a cat."

Longarm leaned out to grab the reins of Mulligan's
black gelding off the branch. "Yeah, well, you only got
one. And you've about come to the end of your rope."

"The people of Diamondback won't hang me."

"No, but a federal judge will. Come on, you're a
law-reader, ain't ya?" As Longarm put the bay back
on the trail, he glanced over his shoulder at Mulligan.
"Trying to kill a deputy U.S. marshal is a federal
offense."

Mulligan stared back at him blandly. Though it
hurt like hell, straining his cracked and swollen lips,
Longarm grinned and then booted the bay on up the
trail.

Diamondback arranged itself in the sage and rocks
ahead of them about forty-five minutes later, a little
after noon. A hot, dry wind had come up, blowing dirt

around. As Longarm led Mulligan's black into town, squinting against the dust, he saw Alexander Richmond and his son, Jack, both in vests and shirtsleeves and puffing cigars, talking with an aproned gent on the front porch of the mercantile on the street's right side. Jack Richmond spied Longarm and his prisoner first, and nudged his father, who turned toward the street, as did the man in the apron, all three scowling.

"What in god's name?" croaked Richmond as the horses clomped past the mercantile.

"The Almighty had nothin' to do with it," Longarm said, staring straight ahead. "It was Mulligan and a few wolves he lured into his pack. Best fetch the doc for your friend here, Richmond. Feelin' poorly, don't ya know. He'll be over at the jail . . . before headin' back to Denver with me."

He glanced over his shoulder. "And you an' me'll be talkin' soon. I still need answers."

Longarm turned his head forward as he angled toward the sheriff's office sitting on the left side of the street, across from the bank and the Diamondback Hotel.

Richmond had to have killed Rainey. He'd known the sheriff would be after Mulligan, and he'd felt compelled to rescue his business partner . . . as well as his business. He'd probably hired another of Tanner Webster's men to pull the trigger.

Longarm swung down from the bay's back in front of the jailhouse. He glanced at Mulligan sitting slouched in his saddle, dozing, his face ashen around his large, red nose.

"Sit tight," Longarm said.

Intending to open a cell door before cutting the attorney free of his saddle, Longarm walked up the three porch steps and reached for the door handle. He stopped. He wasn't sure why. Rainey had been killed here. Chicken flesh rose across the back of Longarm's neck.

He stared at the handle that was an inch off the end of his extended hand. He stepped to one side, pressed his shoulder against the door frame, and then reached out in front of him and whipped the door wide.

The blast set up what sounded like a dozen little girls screaming in his ears. The buckshot had ripped a chunk out of the side of the door and pelted the frame near Longarm's head. The rest of the shot went careening through the opening and into the street.

Before the echo of the blast had died, and before the door could swing back toward the frame, Longarm took his .44 in his left hand, angled inside the jailhouse, and, gritting his teeth furiously, emptied the double-action popper in less than five seconds.

His slugs tore into the office's dingy shadows, the red flames lunging through the powder smoke to reveal a murky image bounding backward, bouncing off the door of one of the cells with a clang, and collapsing.

Longarm lowered the smoking pistol and stepped inside the jailhouse. He blinked against the wafting smoke that burned like pepper in his eyes and nose, and crouched over the slender figure lying belly-down in the middle of the room. He saw the gold-blond hair knotted behind the fine head and, with a shaking hand, rolled her over onto her back.

Meg Rainey convulsed, blood slithering down from one corner of her mouth. Her hazel eyes stared up at

Longarm, pain-racked. She sobbed. Blood matted her cream shirt, brown vest, and man's twill pants. The cream hat was on the floor in front of a cell door.

Longarm just stared down at her, shock turning all his muscles to stone.

Running footsteps rose behind Longarm. He glanced behind to see Jack Richmond poke his head in the door.

"Who . . . what . . . ?"

Then he saw Meg Rainey, and his lower jaw loosened. As he moved slowly into the room, his father came up behind him, red-faced, breathless, staring incredulously down and around his son and Longarm.

"What's all the shooting?" Richmond demanded.

Jack stood staring down at Mrs. Rainey, who stared up at him. Young Richmond shook his head and dropped to a knee. "Meg . . . ?"

She convulsed again, shuddered, more blood oozing out the corner of her mouth. Her lips quirked a painful smile. "I . . . did it . . . for us, Jack."

"You . . . you killed the sheriff?"

"Sure." Her pretty face wore an almost celestial smile as she stared up at the young banker. "Had to. Couldn't div . . . divorce him. Not an' stay in Diamondback. It was . . . the . . . only way . . . we could have been . . . together."

She'd just barely gotten the last word out before the light left her eyes. Her chest stopping rising and falling. Dead, she stared past Longarm and Jack Richmond at the jailhouse ceiling.

"Oh, good God!" Alexander Richmond exclaimed, swinging around and striding angrily out the door.

Longarm looked at Jack. The young man's handsome face was bleached out and gaunt as he stared down at Meg Rainey. He colored slightly when he slid his gaze to Longarm. "We . . . we had a . . . minor dalliance, I guess you'd call it. I had no idea she thought . . ."

Longarm doffed his hat and ran a hand down his face. He felt cored out like an apple. Weary and heartsick.

As much to himself as to anyone else he said, "So she took advantage of the killings of the Bear-Runners to kill her husband. Probably knew about Mulligan's daughter and the Bear-Runner boy. Probably figured it would make a big scandal and that her husband would be at the center of it. And you two would live happily ever after—her the wife of a young banker."

Jack shook his head, placed his hand on his temple. "Oh, Christ, I had no idea she was entertaining such a fantasy."

"Neither did her husband, I reck—"

Outside, a pistol popped. Longarm lurched to his feet and ran to the door.

Alexander Richmond stood at the bottom of jailhouse's porch steps. Mulligan sat on the top step, his back to Longarm. Blood and white brain tissue oozed out the palm-sized hole in the back of his head. As he sagged straight back against the porch, Longarm saw the ivory-gripped, top-break Iver Johnson pocket pistol drop from his hand and into the dirt beside the steps.

Mulligan stared up at Longarm, blood filling his mouth and tricking out his nostrils.

The elder Richmond glanced at Longarm. His bespectacled face framed by gray, well-trimmed sideburns, was stony. He walked over and picked the little .32 out of the dirt and brushed it off.

"We've been in business together for a long time," he said, staring down at Mulligan. "It was the least I could for him. Poor bastard."

Richmond shoved the pistol into his vest pocket and strode in the direction of his bank. Several people had gathered in the street fronting the jailhouse. One was young Ronnie Brown from the Cascade Livery and Feed.

Longarm said, "Ronnie, take these horses back to the barn, will you? Give mine a few extra oats. I'll be pulling out of here first thing in the morning."

The young man lurched forward, gathered up the horses' reins, and led them off down the street.

Longarm looked down at Mulligan and then he looked behind him at Jack Richmond standing ghostly pale in the jailhouse's open door, staring down at the dead attorney.

"Ah, hell" was all Longarm could say concerning the trouble in Diamondback.

He stepped around the dead attorney and strode wearily toward the Dragoon Saloon. He'd get good and drunk, and then he'd get some food and some sleep. First thing in the morning, he'd ride the hell out of here.

Epilogue

Longarm took an extra day to heal in Diamondback. He was just too beaten up to head out the very next morning like he'd wanted to.

But the morning after that, he lit out before dawn. And he wasn't at all unhappy to put the crazy town behind him. He spent the morning trying to figure out what he was going to say in his report to Chief Marshal Billy Vail. When he thought he had it all sorted out, he sat back in the saddle and smoked a cheroot, letting the bay make its slow, leisurely way along the trail.

Longarm didn't feel all that much in a hurry now that he finally had Diamondback behind him. He'd take his time getting back to Denver. He was too beaten up to do anything else.

Late the next afternoon he found himself in the next valley to the east of the basin in which Diamondback lay. It was then that he remembered the girl he'd frolicked with on his way to Diamondback a week or so ago.

That strange, eerie feeling crept over him as he found himself approaching the place where he'd camped his last night on the trail. The place near young Connie's swimming hole.

Why did the odd feeling linger that he'd only dreamed the girl?

As he made his way along the trail, with the stream on his right, a man riding a mule came toward him from the opposite direction. The man was a burly old-ster smoking a stubby pipe. He wore a floppy-brimmed canvas hat, canvas breeches, suspenders, and a red plaid workshirt. The mule was pulling a two-wheeled cart loaded with firewood.

Pensively puffing his pipe, the old man, who had a thick, tangled, pewter-colored beard, bent his head to regard Longarm warily in the gathering evening shadows.

Ten yards from the old-timer and the mule, Long-arm drew rein. The old-timer did likewise, blinking owlishly, naturally wary of strangers in this remote and untamed land.

"Good day to you, friend," Longarm said, trying with an affable tone to set the old man at ease.

The old man merely nodded.

"I got a question for you."

The old man just stared at him. The mule stretched its snout toward the bay, twitching its ears in friendly greeting. The bay shook its head, rattling the bit in its mouth.

"When I rode through a few days back, I ran into a pretty young girl with auburn hair and smoky green eyes. I was just wonderin' if you might know where she lives."

Longarm waited. The old man blinked as he continued to stare at him skeptically.

"I mean no harm to the girl," Longarm said. "I just . . . well, truth be told . . . I had an odd sense about her and can't quite explain it. I was just wonderin' if she lives around here. I believe she mentioned a cabin around here somewhere. Said her name was Connie."

The old man's expression had gradually changed from stonily noncommittal to incredulous. He shook his head. "Mister, the only girl who'd match the one you just described—a green-eyed brunette—did live around here . . . until two years ago. Her family prospected up around Henrietta Pass, just south of here. A gang of outlaws wiped 'em out. Shot 'em all, burned the cabin."

Longarm didn't say anything. His throat felt tight as a hangman's knot.

"The girl, Corinne, used to swim in a hole along the creek just yonder." The old-timer pointed with his pipe stem toward a clump of trees on the trail's right side.

He smiled with one side of his mouth. "Word was she was sorta . . . frisky, if'n you get my drift. Young, you know. Stuck up amongst them peaks with just her family, no boys around. Nothin' but rocks fer neighbors. She used to ride the trails and swim, prob'ly tryin' to bleed off some o' that young sap."

He winked.

Still Longarm said nothing.

"That's the only girl I can think of fittin' that description around here. Corinne McDade. But like I said, she's dead. Dead an' buried with her family." The old-timer looked around. "Unless someone else has moved into this valley. I been here for the last fifteen years, though. I'd likely have seen 'em."

Longarm looked around then, too. Chicken flesh had broken out across his shoulder blades, and he gave a shudder.

"You all right, friend?" the old-timer asked. "You look like someone just walked across your grave."

Longarm's ears warmed with chagrin. He must have been getting daffy in his old age. Obviously, he'd frolicked with a real, live girl. Just as obviously, the old-timer didn't know as much as he thought about this valley.

"I'm fine," Longarm said, giving the man an affable smile. "Thanks for the information. Well, I'll be movin' along. Night comin' down fast."

"As it always does around here, friend," the old-timer said, booting his mule past Longarm and the bay, on up the trail.

Longarm nudged the bay forward. A minute later, he checked it down again. He remembered what the rancher Dan Garvey had mentioned almost in passing about the trouble in the valley east of Diamondback. Another family killed.

Another killing in this crazy country.

Longarm chuffed. He nudged the bay forward, put the girl out of his head. The girl he'd spent a blissful evening with here in this valley hadn't even been close to dead. And he might have gotten a little addled two days ago, but not enough so that he'd started believing in ghosts.

Besides, she'd said her name was Connie.

Hadn't she? He remembered now he'd had trouble hearing her because a knot had popped in his fire.

He found the place where he'd camped before, and he set up there again. He was too tired and intrigued to keep traveling. Maybe the girl would show up at her swimming hole again, and he'd have proof she hadn't been a ghost.

He built a fire, brewed up a pot of coffee, and cooked some beans and bacon.

He'd finished eating and had cleaned his cook pan and sat down on a log by the fire to enjoy some whiskey and coffee and the day's last cigar, when he turned his head to stare off into the velvety darkness east of his camp.

He'd heard something. An approaching rider.

Frozen, his heart stopped, he sat there staring and listening to the gradually louder thuds of the horse angling off the main trail, making toward his fire.

"Longarm?" called a girl's voice. A familiar girl's voice.

Oh, shit.

"Y-yeah . . . ?"

"Don't shoot." The girl giggled. "It's Corinne."

LONGARM

GIANT-SIZED ADVENTURE FROM AVENGING ANGEL LONGARM.

BY TABOR EVANS

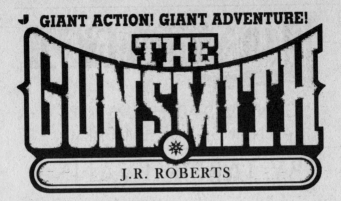

GIANT ACTION! GIANT ADVENTURE!

THE GUNSMITH

J.R. ROBERTS

penguin.com/actionwesterns

M455AS0812

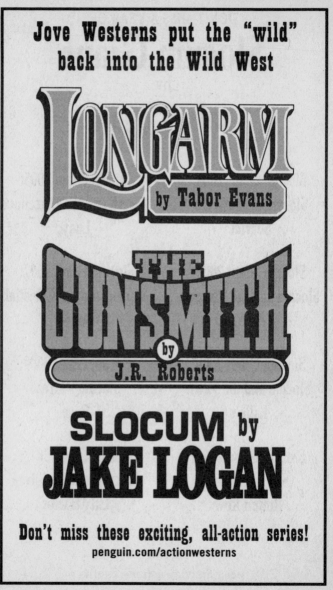
M11G0610